FINDING TRUTH

CHRISTINE GAEL

1

DEIRDRE

It was a gorgeous, sunny day in Bluebird Bay, and Deirdre Eddings had left home early to take the scenic route. Really though, any road in and around her new home was deserving of that term... better to say that she had taken the long way around for a good, long look at the ocean.

She had only just moved to Bluebird Bay proper, and it already felt like home. The vibrant, coastal feel blended with the small-town charm of her early years in Maine, and a good dose of touristy attractions made it the perfect place for her. Home to phenomenal restaurants, a charming local bookstore, and one of the most beautiful coastlines she had ever seen, she had zero complaints.

Day by day, the cloud of doom that had been hanging over her head was slowly giving way to summer-blue skies and briny sea-air. Against the odds, all was well in her world. Her teenage son was thriving, her parents were ready to move into the home she had purchased for them, and she had money in the bank – not to mention offshore accounts, bonds and several airtight bags inside of her couch cushions. She was hale and healthy, as was everyone in her immediate family. This lovely coastal town had embraced her and her son with open arms. So much to be grateful for.

Mostly, though, she was grateful for the simple freedom to drive along the coast.

She had come so terribly close to spending this sunny summer day in a jail cell. The only thing standing between her and certain doom had been an act of mercy from a woman she barely knew.

It was becoming increasingly clear that Fallyn Rappaport, private investigator and former investigative reporter extraordinaire, had opted not to turn Deirdre in to the police for the long string of burglaries that she had committed in a ritzy Maine neighborhood known as The Berries.

She had been waiting every day for the past two weeks for a knock on her door... but it hadn't come. She had hardly dared to hope that she might get away with recouping her parents' life savings from the people who had swindled them out of it. In all her years of preparation, she had planned for every eventuality... including her parents' financial solvency and her son's future if she should end up incarcerated, or worse.

But here she was, two weeks past her final job, simply going about her day like it never happened.

Deirdre hadn't seen Fallyn since the private investigator showed up in front of her house the day she was moving out of The Berries for good. Deirdre and her son, Carter, had been putting the last few boxes in a rented moving van when Fallyn walked up and set Deirdre's heart racing. Fallyn had stunned her by mentioning SkinniQuick, the pyramid scheme that had cheated Deirdre's parents out of everything they had worked so hard for their whole lives... and because Fallyn already *knew* in her gut what Deirdre had done, and because it was only a matter of time before she and that other PI dug up the evidence to support that knowledge... Deirdre confessed. She told Fallyn about her mom and dad and the home they'd lost, about the crank investment scheme that had tricked her retired parents out of all of their money.

And how Deirdre had done what was necessary to recoup what was rightfully theirs.

All that, and Fallyn hadn't turned her in.

Yet.

Twelve days in, Deirdre's hope was still a fragile thing. She glanced at the rearview mirror out of habit as she passed a police car, but it stayed where it was. No sirens. No megaphone. No one was coming after her. She loosened her grip and let out a relieved sigh, but her relief was marred by irritation.

This had to stop.

She had spent the past two weeks looking over her shoulder, peering out her living room window, waiting for the other shoe to drop... and nothing. The tension in Deirdre's chest was slowly unknotting as dread and disbelief gave way to gratitude... but she wondered if she would ever be able to pass a police car again without feeling that reflexive jolt of fear.

Deirdre took a deep breath as she pulled up in front of Carter's school. Her son was busy with a summer college prep course, blissfully unaware of his mother's criminal activity. His expression was strangely anxious as he walked over, and Deirdre worried if her own anxiety was seeping over to her son. Or, worse, if he had troubles of his own that she had been too busy to notice.

Because revenge had come at a cost.

"Hey Mom," he said nervously, bending to look through the car window instead of opening the door. "I texted you like ten minutes ago. Did you see it?"

"I was already driving," she said more sharply than she had meant to. "I don't check my phone when I'm driving, and neither should you."

Deirdre regretted the words the moment they left her mouth. Carter wasn't even in the car yet and she was already on him. She had been feeling the distance between them of late, and nagging him wasn't going to help the situation.

Carter winced. "I know. Sorry, Mom. The thing is, I have a ride... I was going to go get milkshakes with a friend at that place down by the marina."

Keeping her tone gentle this time, Deirdre said, "You should have let me know sooner, Carter. It's a little late for a change of plans now."

Then, she noticed a pretty girl a little ways behind her son. She was standing in the shade of a large pine tree, looking nervously between Deirdre's car and the ground. Carter followed her gaze and gave the girl a quick glance before looking back to his mom. His cheeks glowed pink with embarrassment.

"They were last-minute plans," he said, eyes pleading.

Carter had a crush, Deirdre realized with surprise. Maybe even a first girlfriend. She felt an affectionate excitement for him, tangled up with nostalgia for the little boy he'd been, and a stab of grief as she realized he hadn't mentioned anything about this girl to her.

"Okay," Deirdre relented, clearing her suddenly tight throat. "Can your friend give you a ride home?"

"Yeah. For sure." Carter flashed her a grin. "Thanks Mom. I'll be home for dinner."

He turned and gave the girl a thumbs-up, walking away from his mother without a backward glance. Deirdre sighed and pulled out of the pickup line.

They used to talk about everything... When had that changed?

About two years ago, she realized, feeling even worse. Right around the time that she finally began to implement the plan that she had spent years preparing for... the plan that would avenge her parents and make everything right again. She'd been distracted for longer than that, really. Ever since her parents had lost their house and her father had spiraled into a debilitating depression. But she'd done it. In a masterful series of cat burglaries, she had recouped their money and taken revenge on the miserable people who had driven her father to such shame and despair that he had nearly taken his own life.

Years of learning how to crack safes and subvert security systems, studying how to put her money in places that were truly safe from seizure, making contacts with people who would make it possible for her to fence stolen goods... all of those necessary secrets between her and her family had slowly carved a ravine between Deirdre and the people she loved most. And things had only gotten worse when she moved to The Berries and put her plan into action.

It had been right around the time that Carter started high school that Deirdre had started her search for a house in the richie neighborhood that her targets called The Berries. For the past year, she had been so caught up in implementing her plan that she had failed to see how it was affecting her relationship with her son. Now that all of that was behind her and Deirdre had more free time than she knew what to do with, she saw that there was a growing distance between her and her son that hadn't been there before.

She needed to rectify that, ASAP.

Deirdre turned the radio on and drove back towards their new home, a route she had driven just enough times at this point to switch into autopilot. The distance between her and her son wasn't the only gulf in her life, Deirdre reflected as she turned onto the main road. The truth was, she had felt strangely empty ever since leaving The Berries. Her plan had gone off without a hitch – save for her brush with the insightful and miraculously merciful Fallyn Rappaport – and vengeance was hers. Her parents were financially secure again, Carter's college fund was all set, and the house that Deirdre had found for her mom and dad was currently in escrow and set to close by the end of the month.

So... now what?

She didn't really have a plan for what came after. Maybe she had subconsciously assumed that she wouldn't make it through without getting caught. She had certainly planned for that eventuality, selling the stolen items as she went and stashing the money in a dozen different places. But here she was, scot-free. She should be celebrating.

But honestly? She just felt lost.

And she couldn't seem to keep her eyes off of the rearview mirror.

Deirdre was cruising along at forty-five when the car in front of her screeched to a skidding stop. It crashed into the car in front of it with a sickening crunch as Deirdre slammed her brakes and veered to the right. Her car missed the other car by inches and slammed straight into a tree.

Her airbag deployed in an instant, knocking the air from her lungs. She sat there for a few seconds, dazed, as the airbag deflated. Then, she took off her seatbelt and threw open the door of her car. The world spun as soon as she stood up, and she paused, putting a hand on the roof of her car for balance.

Thank goodness Carter hadn't been there.

The spinning sensation abated, and Deirdre looked at her car. It wasn't as badly damaged as she might have expected. Though it was hard to know if she had done some damage to the underside of her car going over the curb, it seemed alright. She had smashed one of her headlights, but it could have been a lot worse. If anything, she felt worse about the hunk of wood that she had gouged out of that poor tree trunk than she did about her car.

Then, the world seemed to rock, and the white picket fence a few feet away suddenly blurred into the flowers behind it. Deirdre rested her forehead against the tree trunk and took deep breaths until she felt steady again. It only took a few seconds.

"Sorry buddy," she murmured to the tree as she stepped away. "Thanks for keeping me from plowing through your neighbor's fence and into their flower garden."

Now *that* would have been one more headache she did not need.

She turned to see two damaged cars on the side of the road. One had clearly slammed into the other. A young man shot her a panicked look, jumped back into the car with the crumpled front, and set off down the street with a screech of his tires. Deirdre ran after him, one hand in her pocket, and pulled out her phone just in time to snap a picture of his license plate before the car disappeared around the corner.

"Help!" a woman shouted.

Deirdre turned back to the remaining car, where a woman was pulling frantically at the handle of her back door. Her little blue car was so badly crumpled that the door wouldn't open. The woman looked helplessly at Deirdre, tears running down her face.

"I smell gas," she choked out. "But this door–"

Deirdre ran to the opposite side of the car. There was a girl inside, struggling with her seatbelt. Deirdre was vaguely aware of the rapid thump of boots behind her as she opened the door. A strong, gentle hand on her shoulder moved her to one side, and a large man leaned into the backseat. He freed the girl with a single cut of his utility knife, then pulled her free of the car and carried her to a grassy spot some distance away. Her mother followed and dropped to her knees beside her daughter as he set the girl down. She wrapped her arms around her and cried. The girl just stared after the man who had freed her, her face white with shock.

"Are you alright?" the man called to Deirdre. He walked towards her, his handsome face a mask of concern.

"Yeah," Deirdre said, nodding. Her voice was barely audible, and she felt like she was moving in slow motion.

"Come away from the car." He put a gentle hand on her back and ushered her away from the wreck as sirens sounded in the distance. Deirdre's arms and legs felt wooden with shock. The man – a burly, bearded fellow in plain clothes – was kneeling in front of the other woman now, looking into the young mother's eyes with a pocket-sized flashlight.

Satisfied that she was in no immediate danger, he stood and turned to Deirdre.

"How about you?" His voice was calm and kind. "Are you sure you're alright?"

Deirdre nodded.

"Are you sure?" he asked softly. "Your lip is bleeding."

Deirdre touched her lower lip, surprised when her fingers came away dotted with red. She nodded. Took a deliberate breath. Managed to say, "Just the airbag. Must have bit my lip."

They stood shoulder to shoulder as a fire truck pulled up down the street and several people in uniform jumped out. The car was smoking. A police car pulled up, and Deirdre watched the officers step out with a sort of detached calm. She had no adrenaline left to spare.

"Hey Keith," one of the firemen called. "Everyone okay?"

"No serious injuries," the man, apparently named Keith, called back. "Take a look at the car first, would you?"

"Sure thing."

The next half hour went by in a blur as Deirdre gave the police officers her statement and showed them the picture that she had taken of the car that fled the scene. *Look at you, helping them track down a criminal,* Deirdre thought with a loopy sort of amusement.

She needed to go home.

When she walked towards her car, Keith trotted over to walk beside her.

"Are you feeling okay to drive?" he asked. "I can give you a ride somewhere, if you'd rather come back for your car later."

"I'm okay," she said quietly. "I live close by."

"All the same... I'd like to follow you home, if that's alright. Your car looks okay to drive, but it's hard to know for sure without a full diagnostic. I just want to make sure you get home safe."

"Sure," Deirdre said, not quite meeting his eyes. The truth was, she did still feel a little shaky. But she was so close to home... and she didn't want to come back here tomorrow. And she *definitely* didn't want Carter to see her car on the side of the road on his way home, with his mom nowhere in sight.

She took it slow, driving the few blocks to her house well under the speed limit. Her car seemed to be working just fine. She would need to make an appointment to get the light fixed... Deirdre's mind spun with rapid-fire thoughts as the shock of the car crash slowly wore off.

When she parked in her driveway, Keith pulled his truck to the side of the road. He climbed out and walked towards Deirdre, a slow grin appearing beneath his beard.

He was an attractive man, Deirdre realized, now that her thoughts were a little less scrambled. Only slightly above height but very solidly built, with a wide frame that supported serious muscles without them giving him that overblown bodybuilder look. He looked strong and comfortable in his body. His clothes were simple, just a faded pair of blue jeans and a dark green t-shirt. They fit him well. His beard was neatly trimmed, and his dark brown eyes were clear and kind.

Deirdre managed a smile as he walked up her driveway.

"I should have recognized the car," he said with a wide grin. "Seems like you're my new neighbor."

2

CEE-CEE

"AND ANOTHER ONE BITES THE DUST," Cee-cee muttered, staring down at the purple-and-yellow blob that was supposed to be a flawlessly piped iris. She sighed and added it to the giveaway tray. It was nearly full today. She just wasn't in the right state of mind to be doing fancy tricks with icing. It was money down the drain, but at least the food wouldn't go to waste. Every deformed flower was another fresh cupcake for the shelters and food pantries that usually got her day-old muffins. That was something, at least.

Maybe it was time to consider handing more responsibility over to her employees. She'd been meaning to do that for the longest time, but throughout the summer busy season, Cee-cee had been working as much as ever. If she was being honest with herself, she had been trying to keep herself distracted. When she was talking to customers or playing with her granddaughter, Cee-cee's worries didn't plague her too badly. New recipes and intricate frosting jobs usually did the trick too... but today she had flubbed nearly everything she'd set her hands to.

1

How much longer before those PIs found her a solid answer... one way or the other?

Her ex-husband's skeletons were pushing their way out of the closet, and Cee-cee was eaten up with worry about how the blowout would affect her kids. Would it affect Max's bookstore, which was barely in the black as it was? Would Gabe's marriage suffer? His parenting?

Despite taking action by hiring the two best private investigators around, Cee-cee's worries had only continued to snowball. And now, even her work was suffering. Her life outside of work too, especially when the day's baking was taking twice as much time as it usually would. At this rate, Mick might be on his own for dinner again.

"Hey sis!" Anna called from the top of the stairs. "Still underground? You're usually up with the customers by now."

Cee-cee gave her baby sister a tired smile. At least the rest of her family was happy and healthy. "I'm just finishing up an order for a special event."

"Something new?" Anna snagged one of the warm, unfrosted cupcakes that sat on the table closest to the stairs. She took a bite, and almost immediately the smile dropped off of her face. She turned and spat into a trash can, then examined the cupcake in her hand.

"That bad, huh?" Cee-cee was too tired to muster up the shock she *should* have felt at seeing her sister spit one of her cupcakes in the trash. She hadn't snatched more than a couple hours of sleep last night. Her worries had woken her with disturbing dreams, and she'd lain there for hours before she eventually gave up on falling back to sleep and came down to the cupcake kitchen at four in the morning.

"Cee-cee, what the hell is this?" Anna tossed the

offending cupcake into the trash. "Chicken and chocolate? I love a good chicken mole as much as anybody, but this is *not* that."

Cee-cee frowned and looked at the two mixing bowls in the sink, one for her chocolate cupcakes and one for her cheddar chicken and chive muffins. "I may have made a critical error with the batter," she murmured.

"What is going on with you?" Anna asked.

Cee-cee shrugged, still looking at the dishes in the sink. Maybe when things slowed down upstairs, she could send Pete down to the kitchen to finish with cleanup. Usually, she was done with baking by the time the shop opened, with all of her bowls sloshing away in the industrial dishwasher that had cut hours off of her workday. Today, she was barely halfway through.

She had reached the point that the chronic stress and worry was having a marked effect on her health. All of the comfortable jeans that she had purchased since her divorce were so loose that she had borrowed one of Mick's belts this morning just to keep her pants up. Her comb and the shower drain were each so full of hair that it felt like a miracle she still had any left on her head. All of this after only two weeks of worry. If she didn't pull herself together soon, Cee-cee was going to end up bald, scrawny, and out of business.

"Sit down and spill," Anna commanded.

Cee-cee looked blearily at her sister. "Huh?"

"Never mind. Just a minute." Anna stomped up the stairs, and Cee-cee reluctantly dumped the chicken chocolate cupcakes into the trash. She couldn't condone taking *those* down to the shelter. And with a pound of chocolate in the batter, they couldn't even go to the dogs at the shelter. The cheddar chive muffins should be salvageable, though. They were just vegetarian now. She sighed and went back to icing irises.

Anna came back down the stairs carrying a fresh pot of coffee and two mugs. "Wanda wants me to tell you that Mrs. Dreyer called to confirm a cupcake delivery for Thursday."

Cee-cee looked down at her floral cupcakes with a groan. Iris cupcakes for Iris Dreyer. Those were the cupcakes that she was making right now. Three days early, apparently. She'd have to make them all over again later this week.

"Maybe Max can sell these," she muttered, thinking out loud. "They were supposed to be one of a kind, but I doubt Mrs. Dreyer ever sets foot in a bookstore."

"Icing bag down," Anna commanded. "Sit."

Cee-cee did as she was told and accepted a hot cup of coffee. Anna perched on the stool next to her and gave her a long look over the rim of her coffee mug.

"You don't look good, Cee-cee. What is going on with you?"

She sighed and took a sip of coffee. "I've had a lot on my mind."

"Tell me," Anna said in a softer voice. "Please. That's what I'm here for."

Cee-cee smiled fondly at her sister. "I know. I love you. I was going to tell you as soon as everything was... confirmed. Or not."

Anna's face paled. "Cee-cee, you're scaring me. Are you sick?"

"No, nothing like that!" Cee-cee said quickly.

"So?" Anna pressed, looking irritated now. "What needs confirmation? What are you talking about?"

"I have a terrible feeling that Nate may have been involved in the disappearance of Emily Addison," Cee-cee admitted.

Anna set her mug down with a thunk, and coffee sloshed over onto the steel table. "He *what?*"

"I told that private investigator, David Shaw. And his partner, Fallyn."

Her sister was wide eyed. "Told them what?"

"About Mom's birthday party the year Emily went missing," Cee-cee said, staring down at her coffee. "One of her murderers showed up at our door. Chaz and Nate were old friends, but we'd hardly seen him in years. He wouldn't come in, just left when he saw we had everyone over. But then, Nate disappeared. Went out for ice – or so he told me – and didn't come back until the tail end of the party." She swallowed and met Anna's eyes. "I got a really strange vibe at the time."

Anna's face paled beneath her summer tan. "How long have you suspected?"

"A while," Cee-cee said simply. She hastened to add, "Not years, I don't mean that. The memory came to me like a lightning strike... on my wedding night."

"That's grim," Anna muttered.

Cee-cee took a deep breath and continued, "I could be completely off-base, but Nate's been acting *so* weird ever since she found Emily's body. God, I feel sick to my stomach just saying it out loud. If he knew...maybe even helped them in some way, and then came home to us like everything was normal? Or not quite. Like I said, he seemed off, but he told me he killed a cat on his way home from the store. That was what took him so long..." Cee-cee trailed off and took a sip of the coffee, grateful that Anna had given it to her black. Her stomach couldn't take the cream and sugar just now; she felt queasy.

"Have you told anyone else?" Anna asked quietly. "Does Ethan know?" Their sister's boyfriend worked for the Bluebird Bay Police Department; he was the one who had arrested the Bartholomews for the murder of Emily Addison recently, decades after the crime was committed.

"I talked to Mick, first." Cee-cee closed her eyes and took another sip of her coffee. "And two weeks ago, I told Fallyn and Shaw. They haven't found anything yet, but according to Ethan, it sounds like the Bartholomews are angling for shorter sentences, trying to bargain before turning on each other."

"Well then why wouldn't they just turn on Nate as part of some deal if he was involved?" Anna asked.

Cee-cee shook her head. "I don't know, Anna."

"I'm sorry. That's putting the cart before the horse. What a thing to carry, sister," Anna murmured, taking one of Cee-cee's hands in her own. "Why didn't you tell me?"

"Because I don't really *know* anything. Not for sure. I mean, I have no proof. But in my gut..." Cee-cee shook her head. "Max and Gabe don't know. But my heart is breaking for them already. I'll feel a whole lot lighter when this thing is resolved, one way or another."

"Yeah," Anna murmured, squeezing Cee-cee's hand. Cee-cee was simultaneously exhausted and amped up on the five cups of coffee she'd had that day. Her mind spun with memories of her family: little Max running to greet her father at the door, Gabe walking hand in hand with Nate, little Gracie asleep on her grandfather's chest. Every happy memory she had felt tainted by this one horrific thing that Nate had done.

"But when I think about how happy my kids are," she added slowly, "what beautiful lives they've made for themselves... a huge part of me wants to postpone them learning the truth for as long as I can."

3

DEIRDRE

ON THE MORNING after the accident, Deirdre was slow to wake up. She lay in bed for a long while, gingerly moving one limb at a time. Everything hurt. Her whole body felt like it had been through the wringer. Her spine felt all out of whack, and the muscles between her shoulder blades were tight as a rock.

Is there a chiropractor in town? she wondered. The last thing she wanted to do today was get in her car and drive. But maybe there was one nearby. An auto mechanic and a chiropractor. She would find both before the day was out. But first, coffee.

Deirdre sat up with a wince and got out of bed. It took a fair amount of willpower to trade her pajamas out for a hoodie and her comfiest cotton leggings. Maybe in her twenties or thirties she could have bounced back from a run-in with a tree, but today, she felt like her bones were grinding together.

Deirdre paused at the mirror to look at her lip, which was still split and swollen. It stung when she brushed her teeth, and she felt like she had lost a fight. But all in all, it could have been so much worse. Carter hadn't been there. She had been able to veer off the road in time. No one had died or been seriously injured. They had been lucky.

Thank God Keith was there. The little girl in the car was probably ten or eleven, and Deirdre would have struggled to get her out. But her broad-shouldered neighbor had sliced through the seatbelt in one motion and scooped the girl out of the car like she weighed no more than a baby. Deirdre could see him clearly in her mind's eye – the muscles of his arms, the broad expanse of his back – and she pushed the image away with a jolt of shock. That sort of complication was the *last* thing that she needed right now. She doubted that her hunky neighbor was single anyway. *Not* that it would make a difference, Deirdre reminded herself sternly, because she was *not* in the market for a hunk – for a *man*. For anyone.

She gave herself an exasperated look in the mirror. Had the crash scrambled her brains or what? She was more level headed than this.

Deirdre emerged from the master bedroom to the sight of Carter's gangly legs and oversized tennis shoes sticking out from her closet door. He was rooting through one of the boxes in her closet. One of *those* boxes. Her heart skipped a beat. God, why had she brought them here? Stupid, lazy, thoughtless...

"What are you doing, kiddo?" she asked him, trying to keep her voice light.

"I'm looking for my discs," he muttered from somewhere beneath her winter coats.

She frowned in confusion. Her first thought was of floppy

19

disks, but she doubted that Carter even knew what a floppy disk *was*. "Your what?"

"My discs," he said again, sitting up and shaking his overgrown hair out of his face. His frown mirrored hers, and she tried to smooth her expression. "You know, for disc golf. They weren't in any of the boxes in my room."

"Your frisbee golf stuff?" Her voice was still jagged with stress, and she worked to smooth that out too as she said, "It's in a box in the garage. Over by the garden tools, I think."

"Oh. Okay, thanks." Carter didn't head for the door. Instead, he held out a box containing a very expensive pair of diamond cufflinks, his face still set in a puzzled frown. "What's this? Were these dad's?"

Deirdre tried to smile. She hoped that her son couldn't see the pulse pounding in her neck as she shook her head. Why hadn't she sold those yet? She had been so flummoxed by her visit from Fallyn that she'd dropped the ball on getting rid of the stuff from her final haul. The guy she'd been using as a go-between for the past few months was out of town, but that was no excuse for having this stuff in her *home*. She looked down at the ridiculous cufflinks, wishing that they would disappear. Wishing that she had never taken them at all. Had Carter seen the other jewelry boxes? She tried for damage control.

"I saw them at an estate sale and thought they would be a fun birthday gift for Grandpa," she lied. God, the number of lies that she had told her son over the years... There was no end to this. There was no choice now. She had to keep her secrets to protect her son. This wasn't Carter's burden to bear.

"Fancy cufflinks?" he said now, wrinkling his nose. "For *Grandpa*?"

"You're right." Deirdre laughed nervously. "It's silly. They were just such a good price that I thought – but no, you're right. They're so not him. I'll find him something else."

"You're buying him a *house*, Mom." Carter smiled and stood, stretching. "Isn't that enough?"

"What, so he never gets another birthday present?" she asked, teasing.

"He'd be happy with, like, a bottle of whisky. Or a cheese platter."

"Probably," Deirdre agreed with a shaky laugh. "But the house is an investment as much as anything. It'll be yours someday. To rent, sell, live in. Whatever."

Carter made a face. "When everyone's dead, you mean? That's morbid."

She chuckled. "Yeah, I guess. Sorry. Mom stuff. Do you want some waffles?"

"Sure. Thanks. And *I'm* sorry. I didn't mean – I appreciate everything that you do. For me, and for them. Really. I just don't like to think about getting stuff when you and Grandma and Grandpa are all gone. It just doesn't seem worth it, you know?"

She nodded, eyes burning with unshed tears. He was such a sweet boy.

"I'm gonna go find those discs." He handed her the cufflinks and walked away, but Deirdre put a hand on his arm as he passed. She blinked back her tears and changed the subject.

"Carter," she said, "you haven't played frisbee golf in years. Why the renewed interest?"

Color rose to his cheeks and he looked away. "A friend invited me to play. I guess there's a course down by the beach. Sounds like fun."

Deirdre immediately knew that the girl she had seen standing in the shade of the pine tree was the "friend" that he was playing with today. She put a pin in that. It could very well be that Carter was telling her the truth – they might still be in the "just friends" stage, despite his obvious feelings for the girl. Deirdre was hurt that he wouldn't tell her about his crush, but she didn't want to push. He would tell her about this girl when he was ready... or so she hoped.

"Sounds like fun," she said lightly. "Dinner at home tonight, alright buddy?"

"Sure," he said, and then he was gone.

Deirdre shoved the tiny box of cufflinks into her pocket. She needed to get rid of the hideous things *yesterday*. But today, while Carter was gone, would be the next best thing. She'd worry about it after he left. For now, she headed into the kitchen, intent on making Carter's favorite breakfast: Belgian waffles with fresh berries. A call came in as the waffle maker steamed. Deirdre answered it, and her mom's face appeared on the screen.

"Deirdre!" her mom exclaimed, looking so joyful that Deirdre's heart immediately felt a million times lighter. "We just got a call from the realtor!"

"And?" Deirdre asked, smiling. She had gotten the same news in the form of a text message on her phone the night before, but she let her mom tell her the news anyhow.

"We're clear to close the day after tomorrow! We could be settling into the house by next week!"

Deirdre beamed. "That's great Mom! I'm so excited for you."

"Is that Dee-dee?" her father asked. "Give her here."

Deirdre got an up-close look at her dad's ear hair before the picture went dark.

"Is that you pumpkin?"

"It's on FaceTime," her mother scolded him.

"On what?" he grouched.

"On FaceTime! The video! Don't hold it up to your ear, you old goof!"

"Well, excuse me for holding a phone up to my ear," he muttered as Deirdre's mom snatched the phone away from him and held it so that she could see both of their faces. Her mom looked as bright and sunny as her newly dyed golden-blonde hair, but her dad's expression was still somewhat wary, as if this house might be snatched away from them at any moment. When he saw Deirdre's face, though, he smiled.

"There you are, princess!" Then, he frowned. "What happened to your lip?"

"It's nothing," she said quickly. His expression grew darker as she tried to think of a convincing lie, so instead she gave them a slightly sanitized version of the truth. "I bumped into something with my car and my airbag went off."

"Oh my goodness!" her mother exclaimed. "Deirdre, are you okay?"

"I'm *fine*." Deirdre propped the phone up on the counter to take a waffle out and pour more batter in. "I'm fine, my car's fine, and Carter wasn't even there. It was just an overzealous airbag."

"I've told you to sell that car and get something more reliable," her father rumbled.

"I'm fine, Dad."

Always the peacemaker, her mother cut in, "Well, I am just so grateful that your house-flipping business is booming to the point that you could buy us the retirement home of our dreams! I can hardly believe that I'll be waking up to an ocean view every day for the rest of my life. I am just so proud of you, Deirdre."

"Thanks, Mom."

"It really wasn't necessary," her dad said.

"I know it wasn't necessary." Deirdre picked her phone back up and smiled at them. "But this house was too good to pass up. It's a great investment, and you'll be doing me a favor by taking care of the place. I'm excited to have you living so much closer to me. You'll love Bluebird Bay."

"If all goes well," her mom said, "we'll be ready to move this weekend. You and Carter will come help us, won't you?"

"Of course."

"Well, we should go. The Lewises will be here any minute. They're going to miss us around here, I'll tell you what."

"Their loss is my gain," Deirdre said with a smile.

"See you this weekend, sweetheart."

"Take care of yourself, pumpkin."

"I love you!" Deirdre told them. "Talk to you soon."

She pulled the last waffle from the iron and added it to the towering stack on Carter's plate, adding a healthy serving of butter in between tiers. He had the appetite typical of a teenage boy, and some days Deirdre could hardly keep up. Waffles were a helpful staple, and they reminded her of simpler days. Back when she used to cut her son's waffles for him, first into long lines, and then into bite-sized squares. *Twains and caws Mama!*

"Hey Mom?" Carter stood at the kitchen door with a cardboard box under one arm.

She smiled at him. "Breakfast is ready!"

He grimaced. "I'm sorry Mom. My friend just texted and they'll be here any minute. We're going to get breakfast at the diner on the way to the disc golf course. Can I take a rain check on the waffles?"

Deirdre tried not to let her disappointment show. "Sure. Have fun. I'll see you... for dinner," she said to his back as he turned to go.

"Thanks Mom!" he called over his shoulder. "Love you!"

"I love you too!" She turned towards the table with a sigh. He'd left her stuck with a plate for herself *and* his own ridiculous stack. Well, thankfully they didn't have any syrup on them yet. They'd keep. Maybe she'd put *all* of the waffles in the fridge and make herself something else. Or just grab a nectarine and call it good.

"Hey Mom!" Carter called from outside. "Our neighbor Keith is here!"

She walked out front to see Carter folding himself into a tiny two-door car driven by the pretty girl she had seen the other day. They drove away and she turned her attention to Keith, feeling a little giddy at the sight of yesterday's hero standing on her front walk.

"I just wanted to stop by and see how you were feeling." Keith's voice was steady, but he almost sounded shy. Beneath his beard, his smile was warm and tentative at the same time.

"A little worse for wear," Deirdre admitted with a matching smile, "but nothing serious."

"I brought this." Keith walked across the lawn and held out a tiny glass jar. "It's a salve that all the guys at the station use. We swear by it. Sore muscles, bruises, bad backs... It's a cure all."

"Thank you." Deirdre took the jar, and her cheeks burned at the brief touch of his callused skin against her soft hands. *A cat burglar's hands*, she thought severely, dousing the butterflies in her stomach with pesticides. But they were resilient things, and her next words came out with no forethought at all. "Would you like to join me for breakfast? My son just stood me up, and I have more waffles than I can eat."

Keith grinned. "I would love to. Thank you." He followed her inside and took Carter's seat at the table while Deirdre poured them each a cup of coffee.

"Don't feel like you have to eat it all if it's too much," she said.

"I'm not a teenager anymore," he said wryly, "but I think I can manage."

Keith was warmly appreciative as she set out the syrup, berries, and whipped cream.

"So," Deirdre said as she sat down, "you're a firefighter?"

"I am," he confirmed as he doused his waffles with syrup. "Going on ten years now."

She nodded, giving him a closer look. He seemed to be at least the same age as her, maybe even in his late forties. Becoming a firefighter in middle life was no small thing. She was impressed. Keith was cutting his waffles now, and she found herself watching his movements, wishing that she could ask him to rub that salve of his in the hard-to-reach spot between her shoulders.

Which was absurd.

She cleared her throat and turned her attention to her own waffles.

"How about you," Keith asked. "What do you do for work?"

She gave him an apologetic smile around a mouthful of food. When she felt in full control of her voice again, she said, "I flip houses."

"That's brilliant!" he exclaimed. "I've always thought that would be a great way to make a living. How did you get into it?"

"Well, Carter's dad and I bought a real fixer-upper about fifteen years ago. Then, he left me with a toddler, no kitchen sink, and a toilet that didn't work... so I figured out how to do it all on my own. Carter and I lived with my parents for a bit, but I managed to fix the place up pretty quick. Actually, I ended up moving *back* in with my parents and renting the place out so that I could afford to stay home with Carter a while longer. Making ends meet as a single mom was rough... Anyway, that's where it started. I took on more odd jobs here and there. Did some house sitting, got hired by a friend of my dad's as a property manager. A couple of friends paid me to help with their own home renovation projects after seeing what I had done with my place. It all just sort of snowballed. My house was worth so much more than I owed by the time that I sold that I was able to buy a nice place for my son and I, *plus* a fixer-upper down the street... and I kept going from there. I'll probably get another place eventually, when the right house comes on the market here in town."

"What do you look for in a fixer upper?" Keith asked.

Deirdre took a sip of coffee as she mulled over the

question. "You know, I'm not sure. In the past, I was always looking for the best investment opportunity with a turnaround time of anything from a few months to a few years. Foreclosures in need of a facelift, you know? Inexpensive houses that I could put some work and money into and really get a lot out of. Carter and I have lived in a few different houses over the years, since I could avoid paying capital gains taxes by living in a place for two years or more. So I used to look for either places that were a quick, easy flip *or* for livable places that I could fix up slowly over a couple of years in between working on other projects."

She paused and cut into her last waffle, mind drifting to a passion project that had been simmering in the back of her mind for well over a decade now. For the first time in her life, she had the time and the resources to accomplish it. But could she really make it happen? She had been feeling so unsteady lately. Would taking on a massive new endeavor give her the direction and drive that she was lacking, or would it just be a huge stressor?

"And now?" Keith asked gently.

She looked up at him with a start. "What's that?"

"What are you looking for now?" His eyes were intent on hers, and Deirdre felt a brush creep up her cheeks. She looked away and topped up each of their coffee cups.

"Well," Deirdre said slowly, hesitant to speak her most treasured ambitions aloud, "there *is* this one idea that I have... something that I've been thinking about for years. You know, I've never told anyone about it. I'm not sure I have what it takes, to tell you the truth. But I've always wanted to create a community for single mothers. Life was so hard when Carter was little, making ends meet while making sure his needs were met. Or trying to. I don't know *what* I would have done without my parents' help. I watched my friends struggle, other single moms who didn't have that level of family support, and it just broke my heart that I couldn't do more to help them. Moms try to prop each other up, but it can feel impossible when we're only just treading water ourselves. So I've always wanted to create a space for single moms and their kids that would provide them with true support."

"That's a brilliant idea," Keith said. "What would it look like?"

She met his eyes and smiled. "I'm not sure. I would love to be able to buy up a whole cul-de-sac, or a block in a run-down neighborhood, and turn the backyards into one big community space where the kids could be safe to play. Childcare, a playground, the works."

"Like a women's shelter?"

"No," Deirdre shook her head, "not exactly. I don't want it to be a temporary shelter with women cycling through all the time. The idea would be to give them a place to live until their children were grown or until they chose to move out. Long-term community for women who don't have help from their children's fathers or extended families.

"I'd have to do more research to find out how things would work financially. Section Eight might do it, or I could try starting my own charity in order to provide subsidized rent, childcare, that sort of thing. Free rent to start, maybe, with a flexible plan to scale up according to each family's ability to pay."

Keith nodded and swallowed a bite of food. "That sounds like something that would have a huge impact on the community." His clear brown eyes were bright with enthusiasm. "It could change lives, that's for sure. I know a lot of locals who have had trouble keeping up with rent prices. The more popular Bluebird Bay becomes as a tourist destination, the more people decide to move here. We see a lot of people displaced by fires, and finding a new place to live can be impossible for families who have been paying a fixed rent or mortgage for decades. So many of them end up having to leave."

"That's terrible."

Keith nodded. "I know that my ex wouldn't have been able to stay here without child support. Living in Bluebird Bay on a fireman's salary is one thing. Paying the rent as a teacher is something else. If anything had happened to me, our son would have probably been forced out of the school district that he had been in since kindergarten. I'm grateful that he was able to finish out high school with the friends he'd known his whole life. Heck, he's known his fiancée since preschool."

Deirdre smiled at how Keith's face lit up when he talked about his son. "I didn't know you were a father."

"Yep. He's grown now, just graduated from the University of Maine up in Orono. Majored in Forestry."

"You must be so proud."

"He's a credit to me, that's for sure."

Keith was just sopping up the last of the syrup on his plate when there was a knock on Deirdre's front door.

"You're popular," Keith said mildly.

She smiled uncertainly. "I'm not expecting anyone."

"I'll just wash these dishes, if that's alright with you."

"Oh, you don't need to do that."

"It's the least I can do after that feast," he said as he lifted their plates from the table. "But if you want me to clear out, just give me the word."

She nodded helplessly – there was something incredibly sexy about that well-muscled man clearing the dishes from her kitchen table – and went to answer the front door.

It was a cop.

Deirdre felt like she'd been hit by an airbag all over again. She couldn't breathe.

She'd thought she'd gotten away with it.

She'd thought Fallyn had decided not to report her, that it was over and she could shove the past year's crimes to the recesses of her mind.

Apparently, she'd thought wrong.

4

FALLYN

It was a gorgeous day, but Fallyn's mood was gray. She was sitting in the basement office that she shared with David, wasting the entire summer day on computer work.

Both her day job and her passion project were starting to feel like exercises in futility. Despite diving multiple times per week, she and David hadn't found a thing since those gold coins, which felt like ages ago. They were on the struggle bus at work too. Another cold case... or rather, a complication on a cold case that they'd thought they had closed.

When Cee-cee had come to the Seal Pup Inn on that rainy day almost two weeks before, they had been stunned to hear her implicate her ex-husband in the disappearance of Emily Addison. She had no reason to believe that he had been involved in the girl's murder, but she suspected that Nate had aided and abetted the Bartholomews in making the poor girl's body disappear. They had claimed that they'd stolen a boat, which had always seemed unlikely to Fallyn. Cee-cee believed that they had coerced Nate into lending him theirs... or even driving them out to sea.

But the Bluebird Bay native hadn't given them much to work with. She wasn't even certain of whether or not Nate had owned a boat that year.

"He owned boats most of our marriage," Cee-cee had told them, "but I didn't pay attention to that. There were times that he sold one and didn't find another for months. I can't remember the dates. It was so long ago."

And what was worse, Cee-cee had ordered them to work with their wrists bound. She'd forbidden them to contact Nate's friends and acquaintances over the course of their investigation. The woman's gut told her that her ex-husband had been involved, but Cee-cee was adamant that Fallyn and David *not* rock the boat unless they were able to find some scrap of evidence to prove that it needed rocking.

And so far?

Nada.

Fallyn was inclined to trust Cee-cee's instincts, but David wasn't wholly convinced that Nate had been involved in Emily's disappearance at all. Why would he agree to help Chaz and Nancy? Especially if they were no longer close friends by that time; Cee-cee had said as much. Still, the timing that Cee-cee had laid out *did* seem suspicious. And Fallyn was a big believer in that gut-deep feeling, especially from a woman who had spent three decades with the man in question.

Initially, Fallyn had contemplated whether or not Nate might have been involved with the murder itself, but she and Shaw had ruled that out. No doubt the Bartholomews would have tried to pin as much on Nate as possible. If they assumed he was just involved in the cover-up, though, it made perfect sense for them to keep their mouths shut. Nate could add more fuel to the fire if he became an actual witness to use against them during their upcoming trial.

When pressed, Cee-cee had told them that she was *almost* certain that Nate had owned a boat that year... though she had no proof one way or the other. Records from the marina during that time period weren't even electronic. They had tried to find some paperwork, but it seemed like no one actually had kept records that went back that far.

Fallyn pushed that problem aside for the moment as she spun in her office chair, refocusing on the thought that had been bugging her for days. The thought that could potentially lead them to the truth. Did Nate Burrows have a motive to help the Bartholomews? Because if Cee-cee was right about him, he wasn't exactly altruistic. Definitely not the sort of man to put his neck on the line for someone else. So what did those people have on the guy?

Fallyn took a deep, exasperated breath.

Cold cases were no joke. They had devoted most of their time to this case for nearly two weeks, and they were no closer to cracking it now than they had been on that first day. She needed a break, but she made herself push onward while she waited for David to return with their lunch. Her stomach growled as she scrolled through the document that they had put together about Nate for what felt like the thousandth time.

They had been hard at work putting together as much information as they could and digging into his past... but even with David's expertise, cases this old could be impossible to crack. For the past few days, Fallyn had been digging into Nate's friendship with Chaz Bartholomew. They had gone to high school together and had worked together a number of times over the years, each time that Chaz had taken on a new real estate venture. They appeared together here and there in the society pages. That is, they had found evidence of all of those things happening *before* Emily's death. After? Nothing. No hint that the two men had ever worked together again, or even gone to the same functions. Now *that* was intriguing. But it was circumstantial, at best.

As much as she dug, she couldn't find anything that might indicate that Chaz had something to hold over Nate. Of course, it could easily be something that had never made the records. Even something as ordinary as threatening to reveal an affair to Cee-cee. Given that Nate had eventually left Cee-cee for another woman – and then had left *that* woman for the next one to catch his eye – Fallyn thought that scenario likely.

Not that her gut instinct was any help to her in this particular instance. Their last meeting with Cee-cee had been the week before, and they had little to show for their efforts since then. She had no way of proving that the Bartholomews had blackmailed Nate Burrows. Especially with their client's insistence that they not contact any of the man's old friends or business associates. Fallyn leaned back in her chair and rubbed at her temples.

David burst in, grinning at Fallyn with a surprising amount of excitement. He held a bag of burritos that smelled appetizing, but the aroma was marred by something else – something coming from a cardboard box that he held under one arm. Bewildering mash-up of smells aside, the expression on his face was so bright that Fallyn couldn't help but grin back.

Even when things weren't going well in certain areas,

overall life had been good to Fallyn Rappaport. It hadn't been a smooth road away from her old life, but things had been steadily improving for Fallyn ever since the day that she arrived in Bluebird Bay. She had so much to be grateful for. At the top of that list?

Her relationship with David Shaw.

She was so deeply happy that she had let their friendly work relationship grow into something more. The man was brilliant and handsome and – once she'd gotten past his straight-faced workplace facade – he had a rare sense of humor. He had been so steadily supportive, both in Fallyn's efforts to find underwater treasure and in her unexpected career shift from investigative reporter to private detective.

A real catch off the coast of Maine. Some days, Fallyn could hardly believe her luck.

She still hadn't found a place of her own. And honestly? She wasn't trying very hard. Between her comfortable room at the inn and the three to four nights a week that she'd been spending at David's place, she liked her life just the way it was – at least, for now. Plus, she had to admit, she'd never had anyone in her life mother her the way Molly did. It made her weirdly loath to leave her bed and breakfast.

On a personal front, things were going great. And hopefully, if Shaw's smile was any indication, things were about to be looking up on the work front as well. Not that there were clear lines between work and her personal life these days...

"Guess what's in the box," he said.

She eyed him quizzically, wrinkling her nose as the smell of mildew and damp paper assaulted her nostrils. "A dead dog wearing a pair of wet gym socks?"

David rolled his eyes, but his grin didn't falter. "Way better than that."

He set the box down, tossed the burrito bag onto the desk, and kissed the tip of her nose.

Fallyn tore into her burrito and gave him an expectant look, eyebrows raised as far as they would go.

"I was finally able to get in touch with the old marina owner." David pulled his office chair over to Fallyn's desk and opened the second burrito. "A man called 'Salty' Roy Davies. He still lives in town. The man is seventy-nine years old but looks at least twice that age. He doesn't have a cell phone and he hardly ever answers his house phone. So I tried stopping by. The crusty old guy was happy to point me to his attic, which has about a hundred decaying boxes full of paperwork. Gave me a big toothless grin and bragged about how he never throws anything away. Looking at his attic, that's not much of an overstatement. Anyway, I went through a few dozen boxes before I finally found this one. It has the harbor records from the two years surrounding Emily Addison's disappearance. All the ins and outs."

By the time David finished his story and took a man-sized bite of his burrito, Fallyn was wearing a grin just as big and bright as his.

"He sounds like a character."

David chuckled. "You have no idea. You'd love him."

"Thanks for the burritos." Fallyn gave the box by the door a suspicious glance. She could just about see cartoon stink lines coming up from it. "If what's in there is as bad as it smells, we'll need the fortitude."

"You should have seen this place," David said as they ate. "It was like the real deal of what those kitschy sea-shack restaurants try to imitate. He has this extensive collection of fishing floats – the beautiful old glass ones – in all different colors. Found them all washed up on shore over the decades. He has bowls of sea glass everywhere, old lobster traps in his yard... a real salt-of-the-sea old man. He spent most of his life fishing off the coast of Maine, but he's been all over the world. Got a wild hair in his twenties and took jobs on all kinds of commercial fishing boats. Sailed the seven seas. If the little bit I heard today is any indication, old Salty's got a whole host of stories."

"He sounds like a treasure."

There was a gleam in David's eye. "Someone should write those stories down before they're lost forever."

"Subtle," Fallyn said with a chuckle.

"I'm just saying."

"Have at it. Write his biography."

"You're the one who has a way with words, Ms. Pulitzer."

Fallyn harrumphed and crumpled up the trash from her burrito. She'd more or less inhaled the thing. David fetched the box on the floor by the door and set it on top of his desk. A good thing too, since Fallyn wasn't going to let that moldering heap of cardboard anywhere near *her* new desk.

"Ready?" he asked.

"As I'll ever be." Fallyn pushed off of the wall and sent her chair gliding across their little office.

David lifted the lid from the box, and Fallyn pointedly pinched her nose as the smell intensified. He ignored her and dug right in. Weirdly enough, she got used to the smell as soon as her attention shifted to the disorganized mess of harbor slips within. They were at it for an hour before Fallyn finally paused to stretch her back. As she did so, David held up a slip of paper with a look of triumph.

"Pay dirt."

Fallyn's eyebrows shot up. "Really?"

He looked at the piece of paper again, leaning back in his desk chair. "Nate Burrows did have a boat. And a slip for the night in question."

"The night that he told his wife he went out for ice," Fallyn said flatly.

"The very same."

Fallyn took the slip of paper from him and looked at it. The thrill of discovery faded quickly when she thought about just how little that scrap of paper would help them. Another wispy piece of circumstantial evidence. But it was enough to encourage them to keep going.

"It's a small victory," David acknowledged, "but it's not nothing."

"No. It's not." Fallyn wasn't surprised that Cee-cee's instincts had told her the truth. They always did, if a person knew how to listen.

David crossed his arms over his chest, excitement fading. "The boat is long gone. And even if we could track it down, there wouldn't be any physical evidence left that proved a thing."

"There's only one way to convict Nate Burrows," Fallyn said, sitting back down.

David nodded, looking grim.

"A confession."

5

SARAH

Sarah Ketterman was putting her new office together piece by piece, and trying not to let the panicky, overwhelmed feeling fluttering in her chest take over. So what if her office *and* her new house were in disarray? That was perfectly normal, considering she'd just moved back home to Bluebird Bay. It was decidedly *not* a sign that she was failing. She was just taking a little time to settle in, was all.

Yes, she was *temporarily* using a plastic folding chair as her office chair.

Yes, her favorite pair of shoes had vanished into the ether somewhere between her brother's place and her new cottage.

And yes, her ex-husband was very late in sending her the boxes that she had left in D.C.

But none of that mattered in the long run. All of the big-picture stuff in Sarah's life was well and truly in place. She had a lovely home, a gorgeous boyfriend, and an exciting new job – all in her hometown, surrounded by her loving family. She might have a lot on her plate right now, but in the grand scheme of things? Sarah's blessings outweighed her stressors like an elephant outweighed an elephant shrew.

It was time to do what Adam was always preaching, and focus on the positive: She'd had a super productive weekend moving out of Todd's place and into her new dream home... even if things *were* still in boxes. She had gotten a great deal on the place, and she was already in love with it. Not only that – things were going so well with her and Adam, so far. They were taking it slow and enjoying every minute. They had gone on three dinner dates the week before, two long walks on the beach by Sarah's new house, and yesterday she had fled the moving-chaos of her house for an evening of funny movies and Chinese takeout at his place.

Sarah Ketterman's life was coming up roses.

She glanced around the cluttered office and winced.

The roses just needed some pruning. But before long? Her garden would be the envy of the neighborhood.

The sign on her door read *Sarah Ketterman, Partner.* How many years – how many *decades* would it have taken for her to make partner at an established firm? Getting in on the ground floor of a local firm was a phenomenal opportunity... and Sarah was vacillating between exhilaration and terror several times every hour. But all would be well. They could do this.

She could do this. Sarah Ketterman was bright-eyed, bushy-tailed, and dressed to the nines on her first day at work. She was going to *slay* this day.

"Looking good so far, partner." Val stood in the doorway with a potted plant in hand. She was looking chic and professional in dress slacks, with her brown curls tamed into a bun. "At this rate, we should be able to open for business tomorrow or the day after, at the latest."

"Thanks. It won't take much to get this place looking good. It's a great building."

"Isn't it?" Val grinned with all of the excitement that Sarah felt... and with no evidence of the anxiety that kept hitting her here and there. But then, Val had been working towards this day for years. Sarah had been offered an opportunity and jumped in with both feet; her new reality might take a bit of getting used to.

"It's a find," Sarah confirmed. Their workspace was small and cozy, but it didn't feel cheap or run down. The building had been a small house at one point, and had been converted into offices when Val and Sarah were kids. The realtor who owned the building had retired the year before and rented it to Val, who had known him all her life.

"Here, this is for you." Val held out the potted plant, and Sarah accepted it with two hands. It was heavier than it looked. "Careful, I just watered it."

Sarah tilted the plant to one side and admired its intricately braided stem. "What is it?"

"Pachira aquatica," Val said, and grinned. "It's a money tree."

"Sweet." Sarah turned and found the plant a nice patch of sunshine. "Thanks!"

"My pleasure. Hey, do you think you'll be ready to start work tomorrow? People are chomping at the bit to get in and see us." Val took out her phone and looked at the running list that she had going in one of her many organizational apps. "Mrs. Jenkins needs our help with old parking tickets ASAP. There are a bunch of people who want our help writing their wills once we're up and running... oh, and Stacy Williams called a couple days ago to ask for help with the probate process on her mom's estate."

"Wow," Sarah said. "I knew you were prepared, but man. We're really going to hit the ground running."

Val flashed her a grin. "Nothin' to it but to do it. And if word of mouth doesn't keep a steady stream of new clients coming in once all of that is finished, we'll have the seed money to advertise. I was thinking we might even put a sign on a park bench."

"You've thought of everything," Sarah said. Val had found investors, taken care of all the licensing hoops, and rented this office building. All Sarah had to do was show up and get to work.

"Everything I could think of," Val said. "Oh, and look at this!" She led Sarah to the front of the building to show her a big sign hanging beyond the front door.

Valentina Rodolphi and Sarah Ketterman
Attorneys at Law
Walk-ins Welcome!

"That looks great," Sarah said. "Classy, but still big enough to read from the street."

They went back inside and sat down to lunch at the reception desk, which was unoccupied and would be for a while. They were waiting to hire someone until they really needed to... and until they were reasonably certain that they would be able to pay them without resorting to top ramen for dinner every night. For now, they would answer their own calls and schedule their own appointments.

Along those same lines, Sarah had packed herself a lunch instead of going to a restaurant, or even the yummy deli down the street. She plunked her new lunchbox down and opened it up, feeling like a kid on her first day of school.

"What have you got?" she asked Val.

"Strawberry jelly and cream cheese. It's the only kind of sandwich Jax will eat, and I was pressed for time this morning. I should probably find a daycare place that's closer to our office, but I just love the ladies at Sun for Seedlings so much. I don't want to change everything up on him just to decrease my drive time."

"Yeah, I get that. And hey, I love jelly and cream cheese. Trade you half of yours for half of my turkey sandwich."

"Deal," Val said immediately. They swapped and simultaneously bit into the sandwich that Sarah had made, leaving the jelly for dessert. Val groaned with pleasure. "Is that *brie*?"

"Yep! Brie and pesto and a kalamata olive spread."

"You're really raising the bar on lunch."

Sarah smiled and shrugged. "I like to eat."

As they quieted and enjoyed their food, they heard the voices of two women arguing outside. They seemed to be getting steadily closer. Val looked at Sarah and raised an eyebrow.

"I don't think they're open yet, Mom," one of the women said.

"Did you lock the door?" Sarah whispered. Val shook her head, wide eyed.

"It says right there on the sign," an older voice replied. "Walk-ins welcome."

"That doesn't mean–" Her voice cut off as the door flew open.

"You there!" A tiny, potato-faced woman came marching

through their door, looking like a particularly grumpy member of the Lollipop Guild. She looked to be a bit older than Sarah's mom – maybe in her mid-sixties. A woman in her early forties came in a moment later, looking between Val and Sarah with an apologetic expression. "Are you Rodolphi and Ketterman?"

"Yes ma'am," Val chirped. She set her sandwich down and brushed the crumbs off of her hands. "How can we help you?"

"My name is Letitia Pettigrew." The woman folded her arms in front of her in a businesslike way, looking straight into Val's eyes. "This is my daughter, Martha. It's about time you opened your doors. We've been waiting long enough on Petunia's promise of a local lawyer, haven't we Martha?"

Sorry, Martha mouthed over her mother's head.

The corners of Val's mouth twitched. "You know Petunia?"

Letitia barreled on without paying her question any notice. "Peter Kelley and his lot have crossed the line one too many times, and I tell you, I won't stand for it. I will not."

"And how can we–" Val started to say before Letitia cut her off.

"The Kelleys basically abandoned their house more than twenty years ago. Got a new property down south somewhere, and hardly came home to Maine at all. And good riddance to bad rubbish, if you ask me. But now they're back. And not only are they fixing to block my ocean view with a guest house, they are – even as we speak – attempting to build a shed on *my* land."

"They're not going to build a guest house Mom," Martha said quietly.

"That shrew down the hill *told* me that they've already drawn up the plans. And you can't argue the existence of that abominable shed, Martha. It's encroachment, is what it is, and I intend to take legal action. So." She turned back to Sarah and Val. "I need a lawyer."

"Well, you've come to the right place," Val said brightly. Sarah knew that she should share Val's excitement in greeting their first client, but she was more focused on wondering whether she could finish her turkey sandwich without offending Letitia Pettigrew. She had been too excited to eat a real breakfast that morning, and she was starving. What's more, she made a damn good turkey sandwich. And it was just sitting there. Waiting.

"I'm on a pension," Letitia was saying, "but I have three hundred dollars earmarked for exactly this purpose."

Sarah glanced at Letitia's attractive and affable-looking daughter, Martha, who looked like she would rather be in a dentist's chair right now than endure another moment of this.

"Mom, they're eating lunch. Why don't we come back later? Like, maybe when they've actually officially opened for business."

Letitia flapped a hand in Martha's direction without looking away from Val. "This property has been in our family for generations. I don't know much about the law, but I know what's right. And I know what's mine. I need your help to tell those Kelleys to cease and desist with their attempts to *ruin* my property with their unlawful development projects."

Val glanced at Sarah, and they shared a look of wry amusement as they realized that they were about to take on their very first client... basically pro bono.

Well. That's what Val set out to do.

Sarah just thought that they might make a *little* bit of money, first. She sighed and asked, "Do you have any documentation from a surveyor?"

Letitia looked at her with narrowed eyes. "What sort of documentation?"

"Something that shows exactly where the property ends. If you have a survey map of the property, we can compare it to the location of the shed and send a letter on your behalf."

"I don't have anything like that," Letitia said, sounding impatient, "but everybody knows that's my land. Always has been." She looked back to Val and said, "We own from the hammock trees down to the sitting rock."

"The sitting rock," Val repeated with a straight face, as if those markers meant anything to her.

"We'd need to see the property in person," Sarah said.

"Fine by me," Letitia replied.

"Okay, here's what we'll do." Val pulled a legal pad from the desk drawer and clicked a pen to life. Writing as she spoke, she said, "We'll come look at your property and the offending shed, and we'll do some research on your behalf to see if we can find any survey records. In the meantime, I'd like you to look for any documentation you can find."

"If there was anything like that," Letitia muttered, sounding less than certain for the first time since she had barged into their office, "it was lost a long time ago. But I'll look."

"I appreciate that," Val said solemnly.

"Come on, Mom," Martha said in a placating tone. "Leave them to eat their lunch."

Letitia wrote out her address on the legal pad, paid them

a fifty-dollar cash retainer, and extracted a promise from Val to visit her at noon in three days' time before she finally let her daughter coax her out the door. Sarah jumped up and locked it behind them, and Val laughed.

"I'm sorry, Sarah," she said, still laughing. "I didn't intend for our very first client to be pro bono. I won't make a habit of it, I promise. I'll handle this one if you want me to."

"It's not pro bono," Sarah said with mock severity. "It's three hundred dollars!"

"For how many hours?" Val asked around a mouthful of food.

"That's not important right now," Sarah said primly. Then, the facade crumbled and she laughed. "I'll help. I'll dive into research after lunch." She opened the bottle of bubbly water she had brought from home and clicked it against Val's coffee mug. "Here's to our first client. The corporate job I passed up never would have been as much fun as teaming up with you to tackle this Hatfield and McCoy situation brewing right here in Bluebird Bay."

6

DEIRDRE

"Are you Deirdre Eddings?" asked the officer.

She nodded slowly, feeling panicked and numb at the same time.

"I have a few questions for you. May I come in?"

"Sure," Deirdre managed to say. Her body seemed to be stuck in slow motion, but her mind was firing off a dozen different questions all at once. They rattled through her head as she stood aside and let the uniformed stranger into her house.

Why was he here? Was this it for her? Was this morning the last time she would see her son as a free woman? Had Fallyn finally given way to her conscience and turned Deirdre in? Had one of her targets in The Berries realized that Deirdre had worked for them under a false name shortly before their safes were cracked and their valuables disappeared? Did this calm man in uniform have anything on her at all?

"Hey Larry," Keith said from behind her. She turned to look at him, trying to keep her breathing slow and steady,

49

even while her heart raced. She felt as if she had just sprinted around the block. She had forgotten for a moment that Keith was even there.

"Hey Keith," Larry said, eyebrows nearing his hairline. "How's it going?"

"All's well with me. How's Jacob?"

"He's doing fine, thanks. Got the cast off last Thursday. Starting to get his strength back."

"That's great."

Larry nodded, still looking somewhat bemused, and turned to Deirdre. He pulled a pad of paper from his pocket and looked around. "It smells amazing in here."

"I made waffles," Deirdre said weakly. She was keenly aware of the cufflinks in her pocket, absurdly paranoid that they would fall to the floor at the cop's feet like something out of a bad movie. Even then, it wouldn't matter. Surely this particular police officer doesn't have a manifest of everything stolen from The Berries burglaries memorized. Even if he did, he didn't have x-ray vision. Deirdre bit back a hysterical laugh and said, "I still have batter. If you'd like one."

Another burble of laughter threatened at the thought that a waffle would be a sufficient bribe to get this guy to ignore the fact that she robbed nearly a dozen homes in the past year.

What was *wrong* with her today?

There was a policeman standing in her living room. That's what.

"Thanks for the offer," Larry was saying. "I wish I could, but..." He shrugged and patted his belly. "Wife's got me on a ketogenic diet. It's worth a try, I guess. But that is neither here nor there," he muttered, straightening up a bit. "I'm here to discuss yesterday's accident."

For a long moment, Deirdre had no idea what he was talking about. And then, she realized. The car crash yesterday. *That's* why he was here. She could have melted to the floor in relief.

"The guy you spoke to is out sick with food poisoning," Larry continued, sounding apologetic. "He took his notes home with him, and I can't even get him on the phone to get the details of the case, so I thought I'd get them straight from the horse's mouth. If you'll pardon the phrase. I'm sorry to drop in on you like this when you've got... company."

"Mrs. Montoya and her daughter live just around the corner," Keith told the officer. "I checked in on them this morning and they're fine, no concussions or fractured ribs."

"Oh, that's good," Deirdre said, feeling a spasm of guilt for not asking after them earlier. But then, she hadn't known that Keith had checked on them. She was just plagued by a guilty conscience. It was seeping into everything.

"Did you get a good look at the car that hit Mrs. Montoya's vehicle?" Larry asked.

Deirdre couldn't remember a thing about the car. It had been... black? She shook her head slowly and said, "Cars all sort of look the same to me. I didn't really get a good look at it. I could probably identify the kid, though. He was a young white guy with a shaved head. And I got a picture of the plate." She went to retrieve her phone from the kitchen and pulled up the picture.

"Nicely done, Ms. Eddings," Larry approved. He made note of the license plate number on his notepad. She texted him the picture and answered a number of other questions before he finally put his notepad back in his pocket. "I appreciate your help ma'am. Thank you for your time." He nodded to Keith and turned to go.

Deirdre let out a sigh of relief as the officer closed the door behind him. Her legs felt wobbly underneath her, and she suddenly wanted nothing so much as a strong Bloody Mary.

"Are you okay?" Keith asked. "You look nervous."

"Cops put me on edge." She gave him a shaky smile. "Consequences of a misspent youth. I had a few run-ins with police officers as a teenager. There were a few experiences that left a bad taste in my mouth. It's like a Pavlovian thing, now. I don't know. It doesn't make sense. But even when I see one in traffic, I get this guilty feeling. Like I did something wrong and can't remember what."

"I hear that," Keith said with a slow-building smile. "I'd like to hear about your youthful misadventures sometime. For now, I'll get out of your hair and let you get your day going. But before I go, I wanted to ask... Would you like to have dinner with me sometime?"

She stared at him for a moment, too surprised to speak. She hadn't been on a date since... good lord, since before her parents lost everything to the SkinniQuick scheme. Not since Carter was a little boy and they were living with her folks while Deirdre was between houses. She had thought that her dating years were far behind her; men never held her interest anyway. Keith's question had taken her completely by surprise.

And even more surprising?

She wanted very much to go on a date with her handsome neighbor.

So she nodded before she could overthink it.

"Yes?" Keith grinned.

"I'd like that," she replied before she could talk herself out of it.

"I'm working twelve-hour shifts the next three days, but after that I've got another four days off. Are you free on Friday? Say, five o'clock?"

Deirdre smiled at him. "Friday's fine."

"I'll pick you up," he told her as he opened the front door to go.

"All the way over here?" she teased him.

"Yes ma'am."

"Alright, then. See you Friday." She watched him go, letting herself admire his broad shoulders and thick, chestnut-colored hair. Then, the door closed, and she shook her head at her own foolishness. She wandered back into the kitchen and reached into her pocket, wincing when her fingers touched the cufflink box.

Here she was, mooning over some guy, when what she *needed* to do was get rid of the cufflinks... and any other evidence that she had been stupid enough to bring to their new house.

Well. She had three days. Maybe she could do both.

Maybe she could have it all. Her freedom, her family taken care of, and the hunky fireman next door... Could she possibly be that lucky?

7

CEE-CEE

"You ARE SO BORING," Max said, giving her brother's arm a playful shove. They were walking on the beach boardwalk, soaking in the golden afternoon sunlight. Cee-cee had spent the whole morning at the beach with Gabe and Gracie building sandcastles and helping Gracie knock them down. Gabe's baby daughter could sit up without assistance now, and she was fierce with a plastic shovel. Her laughter was Cee-cee's favorite sound in the whole wide world – and Gabe's was equally precious. It warmed her heart to see him growing into his role as a dad.

Max had joined them for lunch on the pier, a fantastic seafood platter that had revived Cee-cee's long-lost appetite. Gabe and Max had eaten the lion's share of the fried food, but Cee-cee had put a decent dent in the mussels and calamari while Gracie slept in the crook of her arm. That lunch had gone a long way towards making up for another sleepless night, and so did the summer sunshine. They were finishing the day with ice cream and a walk. It was the most wonderful day that Cee-cee'd had since the day she married Mick. Practically perfect.

"Vanilla is a classic!" Gabe protested. "It's endured this long for a reason. It's the best flavor."

Max snorted. "It's barely even a flavor."

"Are you kidding me? Look at this!" He held his cone inches from her face. "Look at those flecks. That's the real deal vanilla."

"Always playing it safe," she said with mock disappointment.

"What was yours?" Gabe asked, pulling a face. "Chocolate tahini?"

"Toasted sesame and chocolate," Max said primly.

"That sounds disgusting."

"You don't know what you're missing," she teased in a sing-song voice.

Cee-cee smiled and shook her head. What was it about siblings? Individually, Cee-cee's two grown children were brilliant, mature, responsible adults. But put them together and buy them some ice cream, and suddenly they were like kids again. Cee-cee munched her own bourbon toffee ice cream cone as she walked along, feeling grateful that the stroller she had gotten for Gabe and Sasha was easy to maneuver with one hand. Feeling grateful for a whole host of things, really.

Gabe had given himself a rare day off, and he had booked Sasha a massage and facial at a local day spa. He had also invited Max and Cee-cee to spend the day with him and Gracie. Max wasn't able to get away from her bookstore for a full day, but she did get a friend – one of the slam poetry crowd that converged on the bookstore each week – to cover for her all afternoon.

Baby Gracie was fast asleep in her stroller, fully reclined, arms splayed like a goal post on either side of her head. Her dark hair was so thick now, and her skin had a bit of color to it after playing in the sun and sand all morning at the beach. She was nearly crawling these days, rocking back and forth on her hands and knees. By next summer, she'd be running down the beach. Cee-cee looked up from her perfect grandbaby to her two grown children, who had stopped their good-natured bickering in favor of an actual conversation.

She was so incredibly lucky to have all three of them here in Bluebird Bay.

"I don't want Sasha to have to work any more than she wants to, you know?" Gabe finished his ice cream and tossed the paper cup into a trash can. "She loves her job, but she loves being home with Gracie too. If she just works part-time, she can do most of it from home while Gracie sleeps. And then she can do the actual home visits and shopping for fabrics and all of that when I'm home with Grace. We don't want to put her in a daycare. Not yet, at least. She's so tiny."

"It's awesome that you can both make your own schedules," Max said.

"Yeah, I'm grateful for that."

"Any more news from your treasure hunters?"

Cee-cee winced at the reference to Fallyn and Shaw, but no one was looking at her to notice. They were good people, and she wished them well on their search for lost treasure, but their current investigation was the last thing that she wanted to think about today.

"Not yet," Gabe was saying, "but they found those

coins... there must be more. Actually, I've been thinking about asking if they would take me on as a partner. Let me take them out for free in the boat instead of charging them like normal customers... and asking for a cut of the treasure if they find anything else. Just those three coins were worth *bank*, and there has to be more where that came from. I don't think they've been looking in the right spot, but I haven't said anything."

"You should," Max encouraged him. "But don't they go out, like, three days per week? Can you afford to take them out for free?"

"Yeah. There's not much overlap with the fishing tours, since those usually leave first thing in the morning. Fallyn and Shaw usually dive in the afternoon, after I'm back from those tours. So it's a long day for me, but it's not like I'm losing out on other income."

"That's cool," Max approved. "I wonder what else is part of that long-lost loot she's been looking for. It's too bad it's all underwater. I bet there were some amazing old books on that ship."

"What do you think, Mom?" Gabe hung back so that he and Max were walking beside Cee-cee where the path widened. "Is it worth it? Low risk, high reward."

"It sounds great," Cee-cee said, trying to hit a bright and encouraging note. The mention of the private investigators had her feeling somewhat sick to her stomach, but she didn't want to give her kids reason to worry. "I don't see any huge downsides, and the upside could be major. Just... try to be mindful of how much time you spend with Gracie while she's small, won't you? I know that everything you do is for her and Sasha, but you don't want to work so hard that you miss out on all of her milestones. It's astonishing how quickly they grow."

"I know. It feels like a Catch 22 sometimes. The more I work, the less likely it is that I'll be around for her first steps or her first words. But if I put in more work now, I can save up and be around more for the years she'll actually remember. I don't know. It's hard to balance."

"You can say that again," Cee-cee commiserated. "Parenting is always a balancing act."

"How many fishing tours do you have booked next week?" Max asked.

The pathway narrowed again, and Cee-cee found herself taking up the caboose. Her phone chimed, and she lost track of Gabe's answer when she saw who it was.

Progress! Fallyn's text read. *David found the old marina slips we've been looking for, and we were able to confirm that Nate DID have a boat during the time of Emily's disappearance. AND he went to the marina the night in question. You had said that we might start asking around once we had solid evidence, and this is about as good as it's going to get. So what do you think? Can we go ahead with some preliminary interviews? I'll wait for word from you before moving forward.*

Cee-cee shoved her phone back into her pocket and tossed the rest of her ice cream cone into a trash can. She had lost her appetite.

"Hey!" Max sounded offended on the ice cream's behalf. "You weren't done with that." She stopped walking and peered at Cee-cee. "Is everything okay Mom?"

"Everything's fine," Cee-cee told her. "I was still full from lunch, that's all."

"You didn't eat much at lunch, either," Gabe said.

Quietly, Max added, "You've lost a lot of weight lately Mom. Have you been feeling okay?"

"I'm fine, really. I'm just..." Cee-cee fumbled around for an excuse, some white lie that would ease their worries. "I've been feeling a little under the weather. Working too much, maybe, and not sleeping well. Just hormones and hot flashes, that's all," she added, hoping that an allusion to menopause would shut the discussion down with no more poking and prodding. But Max wouldn't be so easily deterred. If anything, she instantly looked *more* concerned.

"Under the weather how, Mom? How many hours of sleep have you been getting most nights? Have you been to a doctor to run some tests and make sure everything is okay?"

"I have not been to a doctor," Cee-cee said emphatically. She got the stroller moving again, steering around Max when her daughter wouldn't budge. "I do not *need* to see a doctor because there is nothing wrong with me. I lost some of my winter weight – you know I've been doing beach yoga with Steph – and I get up at four in the morning for work. It is what it is. I'm just a little tired today, that's all."

"You're as skinny as you were before the divorce," Max said, walking beside her now.

"Enough about my weight, Max. Please."

"I'm sorry, Mom." Max's beautiful face was contorted with worry. "It's just, after what happened with Grandma Rose... and Aunt Anna..."

Cee-cee looked away. Seeing that worry on her daughter's face just about gutted her. "It's not cancer, sweetie. For Pete's sake. I'm not sick."

"But how can you be sure?"

"You are looking a little pale," said Gabe from behind them.

Cee-cee stopped, turned, and put a hand on each child. "I'm fine. Everything is fine. I've just been dealing with some sleepless nights." At least *that* part wasn't a lie. "It happens a lot to women in their fifties. *If* it persists, I will make an appointment with Dr. Hamilton. But I really am not sick, so please don't worry."

Gracie let out a wail and Cee-cee's heart leapt to her throat. Had she let the stroller roll away? But no, there was her grandbaby, right on the level path where she had left her. Soaking wet and hungry and irate. Cee-cee picked her up, and her screams quieted into a whimper of complaint.

"I've got this," she told her kids. "You two go jump in the water while it's still this warm outside."

"I don't know," Max said. "How cold is it?"

"I jumped in before the sun was even up," Gabe bragged.

"Masochist," Max muttered.

"Hey, it's okay. You don't have to go if you're scared."

Her eyes narrowed. She pulled off her summer dress, tossed it into the stroller, and sprinted off wearing only her one-piece bathing suit. "Race you!"

Cee-cee chuckled as Gabe sprinted down the beach after his sister. She parked the stroller in a shady spot, changed Gracie's diaper, and fed her a lukewarm bottle of milk. Fed and clean, Gracie was happy to simply sit in her grandma's lap staring at a nearby pair of seagulls that was fighting over a bag of chips. Cee-cee kissed the top of her grandbaby's head and pulled out her phone. Her kids were safely distant – Gabe out swimming, Max up to her knees and squealing at the frigid water – so she called Fallyn.

"Hi Cee-cee!" the private investigator answered. "You got my text?"

"I did," Cee-cee murmured. She watched as Max dove under a wave.

"I know it's not much," Fallyn said, "but it's a solid lead. We know that Nate had the means and opportunity to help, *and* that he went down to the marina that night."

"And lied to me about it," Cee-cee added in a flat voice. It was absurd how much that long-ago lie hurt, even when she was happily married to someone else. She had spent too many decades of her life with a man who lied to her face time and again.

"Yes. There's that." Fallyn didn't say what she was probably thinking – that if Nate wasn't guilty of a crime, he might just as easily have been there with some other woman. It didn't matter anymore to Cee-cee whether her ex-husband had been unfaithful early in their marriage... except for the fact that it would be a semi-solid alibi. She would love to be wrong about Nate's involvement in the murder of a local teenager. God, just the thought of it made her sick to her stomach. She tore her eyes away from her children and forced herself to listen as Fallyn said, "We're doing everything we can to keep working behind the scenes and see if we can find some real evidence. And if we could just get clearance to speak with a few people about Nate's–"

"No," Cee-cee cut her off, heart beating with a sudden panic against her ribs. "No way. He can't know about this. If I'm wrong, if he had nothing to do with this and he knows that I'm having him investigated..." She swallowed hard and tried not to think about how upset Max and Gabe would be with her.

"We'll do what we can." Fallyn sounded disappointed. "We won't betray your confidence. But Cee-cee... it was a long time ago. Without cell phone records or security cameras or the ability to interview people Nate knew... I'm not sure what more we can do. I would hate to waste your money. I don't see how anyone would be able to prove any wrongdoing. We'd need a confession."

"Keep going until you truly reach a dead end," Cee-cee said. "We can go from there."

"Whatever you say, boss." Fallyn sounded grim.

Cee-cee disconnected and put Gracie back in her stroller. Her kids were headed her way. She put her back to them and pinched her cheeks, trying to put some color back in her face. Then, she greeted them with a smile and walked out into the sunshine.

8

DEIRDRE

ONE LAST LOOK in the mirror. Their first-date destination was a surprise, but when pressed, Keith had advised her to dress casual. That wasn't terribly helpful, so Deirdre went with the most versatile outfit she could think of: her best jeans, dressy shoes that could handle a long walk, and an emerald-colored silk top that made her eyes look more green than hazel. She had put on just a bare touch of makeup and left her hair loose.

Keith would be here any minute. She picked up her phone to check on the text that she had sent Carter... no reply. He hadn't even read it. Deirdre frowned and tossed her phone into her purse. That was just part and parcel with raising a teenager. His friends – and soon-to-be girlfriend – had become more and more important as Deirdre faded into the backdrop. She had made her peace with that – more or less – and she was glad that he had such a happy social life even after moving so many times... but the boy could at least text her back.

They were overdue for some quality time together.

Deirdre needed to carve out some time for just the two of them. A long drive, maybe, to his favorite beach down south. There was something about looking out the windshield that made awkward conversations easier.

The truth was that they were due for a heart to heart, and on more subjects than just Carter being less than attentive to his phone when he was out with his friends. With the way things were going with Carter and Kadence – Deirdre had finally gotten the name of this "friend" that Carter had gone out with three times in the past week – it was time for a talk about relationships... and for a more nuanced talk on the birds and the bees than the one she had given him when he was just a young kid.

Deirdre didn't miss Carter's dad often. Or ever, really. The man had been barely more than a blip in her life – a whirlwind summer romance that had led to a pregnancy, two years of marriage... and her wonderful son. The joy that Carter brought Deirdre and her parents and even her little sister couldn't be overstated, and she was generally grateful that she'd never had to share him with her absentee ex. But at times like this? She almost wished that she could give old Bobby a call. It was a shame that he hadn't even stayed in contact with his son. Carter deserved better. But that wasn't the sort of man that Bobby was. So. Good riddance to bad rubbish. Deirdre would figure this stage out on her own.

Just like she always had.

The doorbell sounded, and Deirdre pushed thoughts of her son and his father to the back of her mind. She grabbed her purse and walked through to the front of the house with a pleasant fluttering sensation of excitement building in her stomach. Her first date in years, and with a real-life hero. Not to mention the most attractive man she had come across in a very long time. Just for tonight, Deirdre didn't want to think about anything else. Not about Carter or Bobby or her parents. Not about Fallyn or The Berries or police officers. She just wanted to enjoy a night out on the town with her handsome hero of a neighbor.

She opened the door, and Keith gave her one of those slow-building smiles that she was beginning to grow fond of. He took in her silk blouse and jeans. When a long beat had passed without either of them saying anything, Deirdre asked, "So, what do you think? Appropriate attire for our mystery date?"

"Perfection incarnate," he replied, and Deirdre felt her cheeks flush. Keith was similarly dressed, in dark jeans and a nice shirt. He turned slightly away from Deirdre and offered her his arm. "Shall we?"

Deirdre smiled and reached her hand into the crook of his elbow. Keith walked her across the lawn to his truck, which was still parked in front of his house next door. He opened the passenger-side door for her and gave her a hand up as she climbed in, then circled around to join her in the lofty cab.

"How was your week?" Keith asked as he drove down their street.

"Good!" *I moved all of the incriminating evidence from my string of cat burglaries into a storage space that I paid for in cash under a fake name. I even managed to sell half of what I had left.*

"Yeah?" he prompted.

"It was productive," she said. "I got a lot of work done. Finally tidied up after our move."

"Are you feeling settled in?"

"More or less. The house won't really feel like home until I tackle a few projects."

A smile bloomed beneath Keith's beard. "What's on the docket?"

"Oh, a lot of things. No major renovations, just personal touches. I thought it would be fun to buy some big canvases and make my own abstract pieces for the living room. I want to buy about a thousand houseplants, and I need to build some shelves for them. I'm planning to build a big desk into the corner of the home office, one height for sitting and another for standing... That sort of thing."

"I'm impressed. There aren't many people these days that know how to make things."

Deirdre shrugged and looked out the window. She had plenty of skills that normal people never had need of. Cracking safes, for one. She looked back at Keith and said, "What about you? Any hobbies?"

"Oh, sure. That's one thing I love about being a fireman. Three to four days off a week leaves me with plenty of time for a life outside of work."

"And what do you do with that time?" Deirdre asked, letting her tone dip towards flirtation.

Keith smiled again, keeping his eyes on the road. "I like to go camping. Long hikes into the mountains, sleeping out under the stars with no one else for miles around. I took up woodcarving last winter, and I've been enjoying that. I could make you a spoon."

"No one's ever made me a spoon," Deirdre said playfully.

"It would be my honor." Keith pulled up to the curb just

down the block from the fire station, which was only a few miles from their homes.

Deirdre looked at him uncertainly. "Did you leave something at work?"

Keith gave her a bashful look. "I was hoping you might join me for dinner at the station. Our resident chef is as good as any head chef in town, if not better. Personally, I think that Rosetti makes the best Italian wedding soup in the world. She makes lasagna from scratch and her meatballs are just... indescribably delicious. What do you think? Will you come in with me?"

"Sure!" Deirdre kept her tone light, but she found herself second-guessing this date as Keith circled around to open her door. What sort of man brought a woman to his workplace on their first date? Was he a workaholic? Had agreeing to go out on a date with her neighbor been a terrible mistake? How was she supposed to let him down easy if they turned out to be a terrible match?

Keith gave her a hand down out of the cab and proffered his arm again for the short walk to the station. She caught snatches of conversation and laughter and music as they got closer, and when they rounded the corner she saw a banner sign for the *Annual Summer Cookout!*

Thank goodness. Maybe the man wasn't a workaholic after all. Of course not, not if his favorite pastime was disappearing into the mountains for days at a time. She'd let her anxiety get the best of her, that was all.

"Is this okay? I have to at least put in an appearance," Keith said apologetically, "but we can leave whenever you're ready. I considered waiting to take you out on my next day off, but frankly? I just couldn't wait."

Deirdre squeezed his arm, feeling a blush creep into her cheeks. "I'm flattered."

The event was in full swing, and Deirdre felt like a kid walking into a carnival. The air was rich with the smells of grilled meat and funnel cake, busy with the happy shouts of children. All along the long brick wall that was the back side of the fire station there were tables filled with cakes and cookies and gift baskets being auctioned off to fund community projects. Deirdre paused to bid in the silent auction, wondering if funneling some of her ill-gotten gains into the community might assuage the prickly guilt that she carried just under her skin.

"Come on." Keith took Deirdre's hand and pulled her along. "Let's get some real food." He led her past the grill – Deirdre noticed that all of the young firemen stood a bit taller as Keith passed, greeting him with a shout and a smile – and into the building, where there was a long table of picnic food set out along one wall.

"Who's this, then?" A woman in her sixties, wearing a red-splotched apron and carrying a huge wooden spoon, leaned out over the half-wall that separated the kitchen from the common room. "You've brought a *date*? You? Will wonders never cease? She's gorgeous!"

Deirdre laughed rather nervously as Keith said, "Mrs. Rosetti, please. She'll think I'm a pariah."

"Not a *pariah*," Rosetti said in her faint Italian accent. "Just picky. You're a catch, *tesoro*. Anyone with eyes can see that."

"This is Deirdre. She's my new neighbor."

"Pleased to meet you," Deirdre said. She loved this woman already.

"You know he made me this spoon?" Rosetti asked, holding the saucy wooden spoon out for Deirdre to examine. "Carved it himself out of a branch from that pine tree outside."

"It's beautiful," Deirdre said earnestly.

"Come on," Keith said. Deirdre was both touched and amused to see the burly mountain man looking bashful. "Let's get some food."

Rosetti went back to her red sauce. When she was out of earshot, Deirdre teased, "So you carve spoons for everybody?"

"Absolutely not. Only my favorite people." He handed Deirdre a plate and continued, "Actually, I kept the first ten spoons because they were so unsightly. Once I had the technique down, I carved that monster for Rosetti. And I carved a spork for my son as part of the camping supplies I gave him last Christmas. He's hiking the Appalachian Trail as we speak. It's his second time going all the way through."

"That's amazing!"

Keith nodded. "We hiked a lot when he was young, including sections of that trail. Then, we hiked it bottom to top when he was sixteen. Skipped out on the last few weeks of school, flew down to Georgia, and got back to Maine just in time for the start of his junior year."

"What an amazing thing to do together," Deirdre said. She couldn't imagine her teenager giving up a summer with his friends just to hike day after day with his *mom*. "And he's doing it a second time?"

"Yep! The opposite way, this time, north to south. He and his girlfriend – his fiancée, I should say – started back in early June. I think they're about a third of the way through now.

Taking it at a more moderate pace than he and I did." Keith chuckled. "We went through some stretches at a breakneck pace to get him back to school on time. We moved mountains breaking him out early to begin with. He took all his finals in advance."

"Very impressive."

"He's a good kid," Keith said. There was an adoring undertone to his gruff voice that said, *That boy is my sun, moon, and stars.* If Deirdre hadn't been done for already, she was now.

They loaded their plates up with ribs and meatballs and potato salad, then took them out to the picnic tables that had been set up in the shade of the trees. There was a live band nearby, and they ate in companionable silence as they listened to swing music and watched a group of kids try to dunk the fire chief in a huge glass tank that had been brought in for that purpose.

Keith was right about the meatballs. They were tender and savory, well spiced with sage and fennel and other herbs that Deirdre couldn't quite place. It was the best meal that Deirdre had eaten in ages, and she told him so. When they were finished, they deposited their plates in a tub near the kitchen and walked through a quieter section of the fire station hand in hand. Deirdre paused in front of the fire pole, and Keith looked at her with a grin.

"You want to?" he asked.

"I don't know," Deirdre demurred, looking at the hole high in the ceiling above.

"Come on," he said, squeezing her hand. "Everyone wants to."

Deirdre laughed and very nearly declined... but damn it, she *did* want to. "Yes. Okay."

"Atta girl!" He pulled her by the hand across the first floor and up the stairs to the place where the fire pole sprouted through the floor. "Ladies first."

"No way. You first. Show me how it's done."

"If you insist." Keith released her hand and jumped. He seemed to barely touch the pole at all. "Come on!" he shouted up. "Your turn."

Deirdre put one hand on the cool metal and leaned forward. Keith looked rather small all the way down there. It was a lot higher than it had seemed from the ground floor looking up. Before she could lose her nerve, she jumped. Thank goodness for jeans! She descended considerably slower than Keith had and landed gracefully, albeit with one shoe missing. Keith kneeled and returned it to her foot, Cinderella style. Her cheeks felt flushed with exhilaration, and something in her face seemed to throw Keith off balance. He rose to his feet and stared at her for a moment. Then, he seemed to come back to himself, grinning and offering her his elbow. She could get used to going through life arm in arm with this man.

"Are you up for hanging around a bit longer?" he asked.

"I wouldn't mind another beer," Deirdre replied.

They walked back outside, and a woman shouted Keith's name. She ran forward to hug him, and he released Deirdre's arm to pat the woman somewhat awkwardly on the back. Deirdre stood off to one side, wondering what she had gotten herself into. The woman was blonde and pretty and a good decade younger than Deirdre was.

"Sandra, hi," Keith said, looking just a little bit embarrassed. "I didn't know you'd be here."

"Oh, I wouldn't have missed it for the world. We're all here, look!" Sandra gestured to one of the tables in the baked goods area, where two girls were waving frantically at Keith.

"I mixed the batter!" the smaller one shouted. Her older sister ran over and gave Keith a fierce hug, pressing her face into his sternum for a long moment before spinning around and racing back to her sister. Her mother stayed where she was, beaming.

"Hi, I'm Sandra." She offered her hand to Deirdre, who shook it and mumbled her own name. "Do you know this man is a bonafide hero?"

"Stop." Keith ran a hand across the back of his neck. "I was just doing my job."

Sandra kept her attention on Deirdre. "He saved my daughter's life last year. My little one had crawled into bed with me in the middle of the night, so when I woke up to flames I just grabbed her and ran. I tried to go back for Kelly the moment that Izzy was safe outside, but there was this horrific rush of heat down the hall and I couldn't get through. Are you a mother, Deirdre?"

"I am." Deirdre looked over at the little girl who had run out to greet Keith. There was a burn scar on Kelly's neck that she hadn't noticed before, but the girl looked otherwise unscathed.

"So you know *exactly* how I felt," Sandra was saying. "I was circling my house, trying to find a way in, screaming her name, when out of nowhere this fireman goes barreling past. Not a minute later, he comes running back out with Kelly in his arms. Like I said. A true-life hero."

"Again, just part of the job."

Sandra shook her head and looked at him fondly. "And was it also your job to give me enough money to get us into a new place while we waited for the insurance money to come through? No. So the least I can do is bake up a storm for every darn fire station bake sale for the rest of my life... or at least as long as I'm capable of lifting a mixing bowl. It's a crime that the county doesn't provide enough funding to make sure you have the best possible equipment the moment you need it. It's my honor to chip in and help."

"Well, we all appreciate that."

"I'll get back to my girls. You two have a wonderful time. And come on by our table for brownies when you're ready for dessert."

"We'll do that, Sandra. Thank you."

A bonafide superhero, Deirdre thought as they wound their way through more of Keith's acquaintances and admirers. He was basically Batman... and she was Catwoman. The more that Deirdre realized that Keith was every bit as good of a man as he seemed to be, the more she was plagued with a niggling guilt that *she* wasn't good *enough.* This local hero deserved better than a petty criminal.

She shoved those thoughts away as Keith handed her a cold bottle of beer. He *liked* her. The least that she could do was enjoy this wonderful date.

"Hey Keith!" a man shouted. Deirdre turned to see who was clamoring for Keith's attention now – and the moment she saw his face, she flinched. The man was in plain clothes today, but she recognized him as the youngest of the police officers who had come through The Berries throughout the robbery investigations. He had knocked on Deirdre's door, asked her a string of questions, and handed her his card so that she could call him if she saw or remembered anything suspicious.

"Hi Bert," Keith greeted him.

"And Deirdre!" Bert said as he got closer. "Fancy seeing you here! How's life in The Berries?"

"Not a fan. I moved," she said shortly, and then she took a long sip of her beer to soothe her suddenly dry throat.

"Deirdre's my new neighbor," Keith said.

"Oh, nice!" said Bert. "I like this neighborhood a whole lot better than your old one. Snooty people over in The Berries, if you don't mind my saying so. And I imagine it's hard to feel safe with one robbery after another. Been a while since the last one, though."

Deirdre nodded, trying to look normal when inside she felt like she was drowning. She sought about for something to say and managed to croak, "I like it here."

"Ready for a brownie?" Keith asked her.

She smiled at him. "Always."

"Good to see you, Bert."

"You too, Keith. Hey, we could really use another guy for basketball Sunday."

"I'll be there." Keith put a hand on Deirdre's back and they made their way through the crowd.

"Seems like you know a lot of police officers," she said mildly.

Keith nodded. "Yeah, we work together a lot. Part and parcel. Hey there, Kelly! How about two brownies?"

"Do you want vanilla ice cream?" the girl asked brightly.

"Absolutely I do."

She served them up herself and took Keith's money despite Sandra's protests that he shouldn't pay. Kelly carefully counted out his change and handed it over, looking very proud of herself.

"Thank you very much," Keith said. They found a quiet spot to sit and eat dessert, leaning back against a broad tree trunk and watching the general festivities.

"This is delicious," Deirdre said. Sandra had brought a toaster oven to warm the brownies, and they were studded throughout with melted chocolate.

"It is," Keith agreed. After a moment, he said, "Can we do this again? Without the crowd next time?"

"I'd like that," Deirdre said immediately. She let the warm pleasure in her chest outshine the voice in the back of her mind that told her she wasn't good enough for this man. "This is the most fun I've had in a long time."

"The Berries" Deirdre might not be good enough for Keith, she told that disapproving voice in the back of her mind, *but... maybe with a little penance, I could be.*

9

SARAH

"ARE YOU READY?" Val asked as she parked in front of the Pettigrew house.

"As I'll ever be," Sarah replied, half laughing. She headed up the walkway shoulder-to-shoulder with Val, feeling more like a kid paying her strange neighbor a visit than a professional lawyer on a house call.

Would she ever feel like she was on equal ground with her mother's generation? Practicing law in her hometown didn't make things any easier. Who had come in that morning to discuss her last will and testament, but Sarah's third-grade teacher, now retired. Sarah was delighted to work with people she had known all of her life, but seeing them did leave her feeling a bit like a child again.

Val didn't seem to be suffering from any such insecurities; maybe motherhood had pushed her into the ranks of the true grownups. She rapped on the front door with zero hesitation. Martha opened the door, and her eyes widened when she saw them. "Oh. Hello."

"Hi Martha," Val said. "We're here about the property encroachment."

"*Really?*" Martha pushed her hair out of her face, looking exasperated. "Okay. Thank you. Come on in. My mom's out in the garden. I'll go get her."

It was a beautiful old house, well kept up. Martha left them at the dining table and went to fetch her mother. The TV was on in the adjoining room, and an old man sat stock still in a recliner, staring at the screen.

"She's just washing up," Martha said as she came back in. "I'm sorry. I tried to talk her out of it. The, um, litigation. If the shed's on our land, it's not by much, and I don't imagine there's much you can do about the view..."

"The Kelleys know *exactly* what they're doing," Letitia shouted as she walked through the TV room, "and we are completely within our rights to take legal action."

"You're too soft on those no-good Kelleys, Marty," grumbled the man in the chair. "They're nothing but a pox on this town, that's what. Cheaters and scoundrels, the lot of them. If I had one wish it would be to send those demon spawn back to whatever pit of hell they crawled out of. I'd be a town hero, I would. Just like my grandfather."

Martha threw her hands up in defeat and walked out. "I have some errands to run," she told her mother as she left. "Dad's already had his lunch. I'll be back when this is all over."

"It'll never be over," Mr. Pettigrew muttered. "Not while a single miserable Kelley draws breath."

Val gave Sarah a look of alarm that was faintly tinged with amusement. Maybe Sarah would leave the more colorful cases to her partner in future; she'd rather be back in the office drawing up Mrs. Parson's last will and testament.

"Shall we sit down, Mrs. Pettigrew?" Val asked.

"Of course, of course," Letitia said in an entirely different tone from the one she had used with her daughter. "You girls sit down. Martha didn't offer you a thing, did she? I'll just pop into the kitchen for refreshments and be right back."

"Oh, that's not... necessary," Sarah finished as Letitia hurried into the kitchen. She and Val exchanged a look as they each took a seat at Letitia's dining table. Commercials blared out of the television in the next room; Mr. Pettigrew seemed to be suffering from some degree of hearing loss. Letitia was back within a few minutes with a plate of homemade snickerdoodles and two tall glasses of iced tea.

"There you are!" she said in a grandmotherly voice, and then immediately switched back to the tough-as-nails tone that she used whenever she spoke of the Kelleys. "Now, what have you found out?" When the woman was in Kelley mode, sitting across the table from her felt very much like sitting at the oversized desk of a powerful executive.

Val cleared her throat and said delicately, "I'm afraid we haven't had time to go down to the public records office just yet. You told me on the phone, Mrs. Pettigrew, that you had found the old survey records for this house? We came today to look at your paperwork, your property line, and the structure in question."

"Yes, yes, of course, the papers," Letitia murmured, rising from her chair and looking about in a distracted sort of way. "I do apologize. We haven't gotten much sleep the past few nights, you know how it goes. Just a moment, I'll find them."

She returned a moment later with a survey record that

had been conducted several decades before. Val took it with a word of thanks, and she and Sarah leaned in to examine it.

"Just as I said," Letitia crowed, pointing at the easternmost line on the paper. "All the way to the sitting rocks!"

"It does look like you're right about the encroachment," Sarah acknowledged. "We'll just measure today to be sure."

"I am sure!" Letitia said.

"I'm sure you're right, Mrs. Pettigrew," Val said in a soothing tone. "It's just that we'll need the exact measurements if you want to take legal action. Have you spoken to the Kelleys about the structure in question?"

Letitia's expression darkened and she shook her head. "There never was a Kelley who would listen to reason."

"We can start with a letter," Val said patiently. "Failing that, we would need to take them to court so that a judge could order them to remove the structure. In some cases, neighbors may choose to purchase the land in question rather than tearing the structure down."

Letitia gasped. "As if we would ever sell an *inch* of our land to those people."

"We'll never sell!" Mr. Pettigrew shouted, still staring at a commercial for chewing gum.

"Understood." Val took a long drink of her sweet tea. "Shall we have a look outside at the property line?"

"Of course." Letitia led them out the back door, squeezing her husband's shoulder in passing. Sarah paused for a minute on the back porch, surprised by the sheer size of Letitia's garden. Lush and verdant and bursting with flowers, the garden took up nearly all of the backyard. All interplanted with the colorful flowers were every sort of vegetable, many of them in colors that Sarah had never seen before. There were bright purple pole beans, yellow zucchini, white tomatoes... and that was just what she could see at first glance.

"Your garden is gorgeous!" Val enthused as they walked down the path that bisected it.

"Better every year," Letitia said happily. "It's the soil, that's the key. I've turned mine into black gold over the years. Plants grown in proper soil can withstand anything, and they are so much better for you than the anemic things you can get in grocery stores these days. You won't find anything like this at the Hannaford, no ma'am."

"What are those white things on the soil?" Val pointed to jagged bits of refuse sprinkled all along the path on both sides.

"Eggshells!" Letitia told her. She paused and pointed down the line, showing them how it ran all the way around the garden. "Crushed oyster shells too. Slugs won't cross them. I don't mind sharing my kale, but I do prefer to share it with humans. Maybe the odd rabbit. But I cannot abide a slug."

"Right," Sarah said. "So about the..." She gestured in the general direction of the sitting rocks and the Kelleys' offending shed, but a thick wall of corn blocked them from view.

"People think you can just throw everything in a pile, willy-nilly, and get compost," Letitia was telling Val, who nodded along in a polite display of interest, "and sure, I mean, you *can* do things that way, but it's just... Well, it's like just dumping eggs and flour and sugar into a bowl at any old ratio and expecting to make a delicious batch of cookies, isn't it? There's a *science* to it, to doing it the *right* way. Though, if you want to get *real* black gold, what you need is *vermi*compost..."

In the end, they got a free forty-minute lesson on gardening in Maine before they actually made it past the corn. Sarah felt frustrated at first, but she actually found herself listening with interest to some of it. She was a homeowner now, and she had inherited a beautiful flower garden. She did want to know how to take care of it, and Letitia Pettigrew was a treasure trove of knowledge with decades of experience and an impressive green thumb. What's more, she was very nearly likable when she wasn't talking about the Kelleys. By the end of the lecture, Sarah was feeling inspired to plant some vegetables among her flowers next spring; Letitia's garden was even more beautiful than Sarah's, and it was brimming with healthy food.

When they did finally make it down to the back of the property with their survey paper, it was obvious that Letitia was right: the new shed *was* well over the line. As they stood there, a man in his forties walked towards the shed with a fresh load of lumber. He was handsome, with a well-tanned face and salt-and-pepper hair. An old man trailed close behind him, critiquing his every move.

"Don't put it *there*, Waylon!" he exclaimed, waving his cane towards the lumber. "They'll get wet and the wood will warp!"

"Not between now and when we use it, Dad." Waylon's beleaguered tone reminded Sarah of Martha Pettigrew.

Letitia spat on the ground near the elder Mr. Kelley's feet – which Sarah had to admit was kind of impressive, given how far apart they were standing – and the old man turned away, pointedly ignoring her and muttering under his breath about Pettigrews.

"You might as well stop working on that pile of rubbish you call a shed, Peter Kelley," Letitia told him with gleeful malevolence. His face began to turn red as she continued, "I've got *two* lawyers here, and they say that this unlawful building is as good as done for."

"Well, we didn't exactly–" Val began, but Letitia ignored her.

"We have the official survey papers to show that you have quite literally crossed the line. Isn't that right, Sarah?"

"I'm not afraid of your two-bit shysters!" Peter shouted before Sarah could respond. "I have a *real* lawyer."

"Dad, please," Waylon tried. The rest of what he said was lost to more shouts from the elder Mr. Kelley.

"We have the *actual, official* survey that shows the *true* property line, back to when my granddaddy made the softhearted mistake of selling to that worthless scum of a Pettigrew. I will have you know that you are currently standing on *my* property, Letitia!"

"Of all the ridiculous–" Letitia started.

"Get back!" Peter shouted, swinging his cane like a club. "Get off of my land, you shrill-voiced witch!"

"Dad, *please*," Waylon tried again.

"Go get those papers this minute!" Peter shouted at his son.

"Dad, this really isn't–"

"Fine!" Peter threw down the hammer he was holding and stormed off towards his house. "I'll get them myself! Incompetent, lily-livered..."

Waylon gave Val and Sarah an apologetic look as his dad stormed off. "I'm really sorry."

"The survey map does say that the property line is even with those rocks, there," Val said apologetically, pointing to the sitting rocks that stood just behind the shed.

Waylon spread his hands and gave Val a helpless look. "Our survey puts the line right about where you're standing. We did our due diligence before we leveled this piece of ground for the shed. I'm not sure where the mix-up is."

"A mix-up, he says." Letitia's tone was venomous. "As if this wasn't the plan all along, chipping away at our property a few feet at a time. I won't have it!"

"Mrs. Pettigrew, I didn't–"

"Don't you speak to me, boy!"

Waylon let out a heavy sigh and looked back to the Kelley house as his father threw the back door open with a bang. He shuffled towards them at top speed, working his cane with one hand and brandishing some papers in the other.

"Here!" he crowed as he reached them. "You see?"

Val took the papers that he held out, and Sarah leaned towards her to read. Waylon was right. *This* official survey put the property line just past the location of the shed. She sighed and shook her head. Things just got a lot more complicated.

"We'll have to do a bit more research and get back to you, Mrs. Pettigrew," Val murmured.

"Nonsense. The crazy old man probably had some scoundrel forge the thing. You know they can do anything with computers these days. It's nothing but a piece of trash." Letitia tried to tear the papers away from Val, who jumped back in surprise.

"Back, devil woman!" Peter shouted. He swung his cane back and forth, shuffling progressively closer to Letitia. Waylon put a hand on his shoulder and said something quietly into his ear, trying to talk him down.

Sarah bit her lip as Val talked to Letitia, trying to coax her back up the hill to her house. These people were crazy, but at least they weren't boring. She couldn't wait for dinner with Adam to tell him the whole tale – names redacted, of course. Peter finally quieted, but he refused to budge. He stood right on the spot where *his* survey told him that his property ended, glaring at Letitia as Val walked the old woman back up the hill, distracting her with questions about her garden.

Sarah snapped a picture of the Kelleys' survey papers with her phone and handed them back to Peter Kelley. She smiled at Waylon and said, "We'll look into it and let you know what we find."

"We already *know* what you'll find," Peter said darkly. He walked back towards his house, muttering all the while about lawyers barely out of diapers thinking that they had any right to tell him where his own property began and ended.

"If I give you my number," Waylon said, "would you please tell me as soon as you find something?"

"Of course." Sarah put his number into her phone before following Val and Letitia up the hill. With Peter Kelley out of sight and her garden foremost on her mind, Letitia was all sweetness again.

"You'll take a big basket of veggies home for that beautiful baby of yours, won't you?" she was saying to Val. "They're the best in the county, nothing better for a growing boy. Do you know the secret for getting any sort of vegetable into a picky eater?"

"What's that?" Val asked.

"You simmer them all in tomato sauce. Summer squash, carrots, eggplant, cauliflower. Anything you like. Then, you blend it smooth as can be and pour it over spaghetti. Works every time."

Val smiled brightly. "He does love spaghetti."

"Of course he does. You wait just a moment and I'll make you each a basket." Letitia looked at Sarah and pursed her lips. "You do cook, don't you dear?"

Sarah tried not to laugh and mostly succeeded. With only a slight tremor in her voice she said, "Yes, I cook."

"Oh, good. That's good. So many young people these days don't know how to do a thing that matters anymore. Can't mend a hem or make a stew. It's a crying shame, is what it is. You two just wait right here. Pick yourselves some flowers, if you like. You see those orange ones there, just on the other side of the walking stick kale? Take some of those giant marigolds. There's nothing like a fresh bouquet to brighten a table. I'll just get a couple harvest baskets. You will bring them back to me next time you come, won't you?"

"Yes, Mrs. Pettigrew," Val said.

"Good. That's good. You just wait here," she said, and bustled back up to the house.

As soon as Sarah and Val looked at each other, they burst into laughter. Val clamped a hand over her mouth, looking up the hill at the retreating form of Letitia Pettigrew. Then, she looked back to Sarah and giggled again.

"Any regrets?" she asked, only half joking.

"No way!" Sarah said. "Look at us. Outside in the summer sun, getting paid in vegetables."

"And flowers," Val added. "Look at these marigolds! They're bigger than my fist!"

"One thing I can say for this case," Sarah told her with a smile. "It's way more fun than corporate law."

10

DEIRDRE

Ol' reliable or fire engine red, that was a question.

Deirdre was getting ready for her second date with Keith – and for the second time, he hadn't told her where they were going. All that he had told her was that she would need a bathing suit. Deirdre was surprised to discover how much she liked surprises... at least, when they were arranged by someone she could trust. After a lifetime of planning out every day by herself and managing her son's ever-changing schedule all on her own, it was a pleasure to hand over the reins for an afternoon and let someone else handle the decisions and logistics of a day out. It did leave her with just a little bit of anxiety on the clothes front, though.

Her phone chimed and she paused to check it. It was Carter, asking if he could join his friends for dinner on the wharf. He was out the door already for a full day: he planned to spend the morning at the skate park with friends and then the rest of the day at the beach with Kadence – whom he still stubbornly referred to as a "friend"... and Deirdre hadn't pushed back on that... yet. She was grateful that her son had such a happy social life. At the same time, she felt like she was missing out on what little time they had left together. Who knew how far away he would move for college... or if they would ever even live in the same town again when he was done with high school. But it wasn't Carter's fault that she had missed out on so much over the past few years, and she wouldn't help anything by clinging too tight to him now that *she* had too much free time on her hands.

Deirdre sent him a quick affirmative and set her phone down. It was just as well. Maybe she and Keith could have dinner together after whatever he had planned for today. As much as Deirdre wanted to hoard every minute with her son, she needed to take some time to create a vibrant life for *herself* too. She had just closed the door on a long, dark – albeit successful – chapter of her life. Now was the time to build something new – and not just on the relationship front.

She needed a project. Ideally, something more meaningful than simply flipping another house, driving the price up and handing it over to some well-to-do young couple. She wanted to transform a neighborhood for the better... but as well off as Deirdre was these days, buying and transforming an entire dead-end street or city block in Bluebird Bay was well beyond her means. A project of that scope would have to wait until Carter had graduated and she *really* had too much time on her hands. Then, she could find an area that was truly down and out and buy a group of buildings for cheap in order to transform them into something new. It would be easy enough to go back and forth between managing the project and spending time with her parents... and if the project happened to be close to Carter's college, so much the better. It would be just what she needed to occupy her time once she was an empty nester.

Today, though, she would place both her career and her familial concerns on the back burner. Today, she had a date. So. Which would it be?

Her old reliable one-piece bathing suit in a faded shade of black? Or the bright red two-piece she had picked up on a whim the day before? It fit perfectly, but was it maybe a little too *Look at Me!* for Deirdre's taste... But goodness, it was flattering. Both the cut and the color suited her perfectly. It had earned her a wolf-whistle from the young woman behind the counter in the swimsuit shop, which had made Deirdre laugh. If it was a sales tactic, it had worked wonders. But the sweet girl had seemed earnest enough. So she'd taken the plunge – it had been nearly a decade since she'd splurged on a new bathing suit – and she didn't regret it. But was she really going to wear it *today*? It was so... *bold*. Even so, Deirdre tried it on again and looked at herself in the mirror. The girl's whistle echoed in her head, and she smiled.

You know what? Screw it. Deirdre threw caution to the wind and gave herself permission to be bold. She grabbed a navy-blue cotton dress and threw it over the suit before she could change her mind. If she couldn't wear her fire engine red swimsuit out on a date with the handsome firefighter next door, then what was the point? Deirdre had every intention of taking this new relationship slowly – she had been single for so long that even a second date felt like a big deal – but goodness, the man deserved a *little* encouragement, didn't he?

Deirdre's phone rang and she grabbed it, expecting Carter or her mom... but no. All of her excitement drained away, leaving her nerves about her suit and today's date feeling trivial and ridiculous. She felt a familiar tide of guilt and fear rise in her chest and tried to swallow it down.

It wasn't a saved contact, but it was a number that Deirdre knew well. It belonged to Ned, the guy who had moved stolen goods for Deirdre nearly a dozen times in as many months. She didn't want to talk to him. Not today. She let the call go to voicemail and then played the message the moment it came through.

"Hey Dee, it's Ned," came his gruff voice. He was a reliable guy, closer to her dad's age than hers, and Deirdre trusted him. She was grateful for his help, and forever endeared to the man since she'd discovered that the extra money he earned fencing stolen goods for her – never a question asked – went to taking care of his granddaughter. Still, she didn't want to think about any of that today.

"I just got your message," he continued. "I'm upstate all month with my family. There's no reception at the cabin, so I can only check my messages when I'm in town. Anyhow, I won't be back for a couple more weeks. I can help you then, if you need. Enjoy the rest of your summer, kid."

The recording ended and Deirdre sat down on her bed, feeling deflated. She had moved the last of her stolen goods to a safe location, but she so badly wanted to be rid of them. She'd been itching to put some of that money to good use, and if she couldn't tackle a big project for a couple more years yet... Well, she'd gotten it into her mind that she could take the cash from this final round of stuff and put it towards a good cause. Assuage her guilt in the meantime.

There was a firm knock on her door, and Deirdre pushed those thoughts away. Today was a good day. She would make sure to be present and enjoy every moment of it. Her worries weren't pressing. They would keep. She could deal with them tomorrow, in the hours she spent rattling around her new house alone. Today, she had a *date*.

Keith smiled when she opened the door, and Deirdre smiled back. He bent down and greeted her with a kiss on the cheek. His thick beard was surprisingly soft on her skin – and in that moment, Deirdre's worries well and truly fled her mind.

"Ready?" Keith asked.

Deirdre smiled and nodded, ready to follow him out the door without a second thought. Then, she remembered herself and laughed, stepping backwards. She grabbed her oversized purse – stuffed with a quick-dry towel and sunglasses and a bottle of lemonade – and turned to Keith with a smile.

"Ready."

The drive was longer than Deirdre had expected, but she didn't mind. It was a glorious late summer day, and the drive up the coast was beautiful. When Keith turned inland, she realized that a beach day wasn't what he had in mind. A day at the lake, then? Deirdre didn't ask. She hadn't known her neighbor for very long at all, but she trusted him. And honestly, she was enjoying the excitement of motoring along without knowing where they were headed.

"Any luck on your real estate search?" Keith asked as he drove through the lush greenery of the Maine woods.

"Nothing yet," Deirdre told him, "but I haven't been looking too hard. We just closed on the place that I found for my parents, and I needed a bit of a breather. Looking at listings, though, I realized that I won't be able to afford the kind of place that I would need for a project of that size. Not here in Bluebird Bay. And that's fine. I need to spend more time with my son while he's still around."

"Do you?" Keith asked.

She looked at him sideways. "Well, yeah. I've been so busy with work the past few years, and he'll be gone before I can blink. I don't want to fritter away the time I have left."

"Would you accept just a smidge of advice from someone whose son is grown and gone?"

"Sure," Deirdre said.

"It's not the amount of time that matters at this age. Luckily. They're in school all day and then they want to be with their friends every minute they're not."

"Says the man whose son opted to spend an entire summer hiking with him."

"I got lucky." Keith chuckled and added, "But if you think it was all sunshine and roses hiking thousands of miles together, you're mistaken. There were plenty of times we didn't like each other much at all. But that summer aside, I really didn't see him much. He spent most nights at his mom's place and most of his free time with his friends. So when I did get a rare day with him, or a full weekend, I made it count."

"Quality over quantity," Deirdre murmured thoughtfully. At the moment, she wasn't exactly hitting the mark on either one.

"That's the ticket." Keith turned off of the road and pulled into a crowded parking lot. Deirdre hoped very much that they wouldn't be hiking for miles to reach some alpine lake; she had *not* worn the right shoes for that sort of excursion. So much for surprise destinations.

"Is it very far?" she asked as they walked through the dirt lot.

Keith chuckled and shook his head. "No. Look there."

They rounded a bend in the trail, and it opened up to reveal a gorgeous view. For the second time that day, all of Deirdre's worries went out of her head. They stood on the shore of a huge lake, deep blue and sparkling under a bright cerulean sky. Rolling hills covered in dark green forests covered the opposite shore. Despite its beauty, it wasn't a peaceful scene. The air was filled with happy shouts, and the distant buzz of motors as boats and jet skis sped across the surface of the lake.

"My friend let me borrow his boat for the day," Keith told her, pulling a second set of keys out of his pocket. "Are you up for a ride?"

Deirdre smiled up at him. "Absolutely."

They walked hand in hand along the shady lakeshore until they reached a small marina where several speed boats were moored. Keith leapt onto one called the Earnshaw, then turned and held a hand out to Deirdre. She stepped lightly across and onto the deck of the little boat. They made their way to deeper waters in short order, the boat's engine humming pleasantly rather than roaring like many she'd been in before. Some other boaters came into view in the distance, but the lake was large enough that they had a large area to themselves.

Keith grinned as he let the boat come to a stop, shutting off the engine. "I'm not sure if you're up for it," he started, making his way past her seat to the back of the boat, "but I thought maybe we could try some water skiing."

Deirdre's mind danced back to a dozen happy memories.

Her father had taken her many times when she was young, and she'd done the same with Carter once he was old enough. She opened her mouth to tell Keith as much, but cut off when he turned back around and began speaking again.

"So, if you're interested, I can show you how."

She grinned. "Sure, sounds good."

He waved her over to the back of the boat, waving the skis in front of him. "So you're going to start by laying back in the water," he said, laying down on the ground and pulling his knees toward his chest. "Sort of like this. Your skis will be pointing toward the sky, and your legs should be about shoulder width apart."

Deirdre nodded, hoping she was giving off earnest, studious vibes. "Okay, what next?"

"You can call for me to start the boat once you're ready, and you have to focus on keeping those knees bent while it pulls you to a standing position," he said, waving her over as he stood. "Here, let me show you."

She stepped over, turning her back to him, and he positioned her correctly, having her bend at the knees and keep her body leaned back.

Electricity seemed to spark through her as he tapped her knee. "Just a little bit more."

She let her knees bend a final few inches, and her back brushed against his broad chest. "Good?" she asked.

He stepped back to get a look, then nodded approvingly. "You're probably going to feel like you want to tug on the rope to pull yourself up, but you'll fall if you do. It's just about keeping the right posture. You can straighten your legs most of the way once you're standing."

"Roger that, Captain."

"So do you want to try? You'll probably fall a few times before you get the hang of it, but it doesn't hurt much. Probably better that you experience it than have me keep explaining it all. Just remember this; give me a thumbs up to speed up or a thumbs down to slow down."

Deirdre nodded, and put on the life vest before getting into the water and swimming a few feet out to put the skis on. She pulled back into the familiar position and called for Keith to start the engine.

He shot her a thumbs up and the Earnshaw hummed into action, beginning to slice through the water once again. It picked up speed rapidly and, before long, she was easing into the standing position, letting the boat do the work.

She let out a laugh as they barreled through the deep lake, the wind buffeting her face. Keith turned around every few seconds, mouthing words she couldn't hear, and his face was more and more shocked each time.

Deciding it was time to drop the charade, she shot him a big thumbs up and leaned sideways, balancing perfectly as she skipped over the side of the boat's wake and then back into it. His look of pure shock egging her on, she whirled around, passing the handle of the rope behind her back. Her legs wobbled but she managed to recover, continuing to ski backwards for a few seconds before completing the spin and facing front once again.

She grinned, shooting him the thumbs down signal to slow down.

He slowed to a stop before long, and Keith whistled and clapped as he pulled the boat up next to her. "How did I do?" she asked, beaming.

"That was incredible!"

"I had a good teacher," she said teasingly.

"I'm sure you did, but it definitely wasn't me." He chuckled, reaching down to help her back onto the boat. "So fess up...where'd you learn to ski like that?"

"My dad was pretty into it when I was younger, so he took me on his boat a lot of times," she said once she was on board, grinning widely after her harmless prank. "I know how to drive the boat too, if you want next?"

He put his hands up. "Wouldn't want to follow that act. At least, not yet. Why don't we enjoy the water a bit and have a cold drink?"

They drank every drop of the lemonade that Deirdre had packed, plus the iced tea that Keith had brought. They also ate the granola bars that lived at the bottom of Deirdre's purse, and she found herself wishing that she had brought more food. All the same, it was an amazing day. They would be able to stop somewhere on the way home for a proper meal.

Right around the point when Deirdre's muscles were starting to burn and her skin was threatening to do the same, Keith drove them back to the docks. He secured the boat and walked Deirdre back along the lakeshore to the shady parking lot where he had left his truck.

"That was a perfect day," Deirdre said with feeling. "Thank you."

"I wasn't quite ready to call it quits just yet," Keith said in a quiet rumble. He reached into the back of his truck and revealed a hidden cooler and beach blanket. "Do you have time to stay a while longer?"

"Absolutely, I do," she said with a smile.

"Although, I might be pressing my luck," he said with a

straight face even as he lifted the cooler out of the truck and tucked the blanket under his arm. "I'm not sure I can top perfection, so maybe we should quit while we're ahead."

Deirdre bumped her hip playfully against his as he took her hand. "I'll risk it."

They walked back to the lakeshore and Keith led her in the opposite direction this time, away from the noisy docks and the busiest part of the lake. They followed the path until they reached a narrower corner of the lake that the speedboats avoided, and Keith spread out his picnic blanket on a little two-person beach nestled between the rocks and trees.

"What's for dinner?" Deirdre asked.

"Well, I warned you that I'm not much of a cook." Keith's eyes sparkled playfully. "But I do like to eat."

He took out a small cutting board and a pocketknife first, then laid out their feast one item at a time. It was all prepackaged food – but Deirdre was pleased to see that the man had good taste. There was a local salami studded with fennel seeds, swiss cheese, sharp cheddar, and an herby brie with peppery crackers. He'd also included fresh sourdough bread, a small jar of olives, a savory pepper jam, bright yellow carrots, sliced cucumbers, and a tub of hummus.

"Cooking is overrated," Deirdre decided.

Keith smiled at her. "I can grill. And I can shop. Everything else is beyond me."

"Well, we certainly won't starve." Deirdre grabbed one of the peppery crackers and swiped it through the hummus. "This looks fantastic."

He had managed to fit a four-pack of artisan beer into his little cooler, as well, and they took their time enjoying the picnic feast. Everything that Keith had chosen was intensely flavorful and of phenomenal quality, and it was the best meal that Deirdre had tasted since Rosetti's meatballs. As they walked back hand in hand, Keith asked if they could do this again soon.

"After my next stretch of work days?" he suggested. "Five more days and I'm a free man again."

"For sure," Deirdre said, pressing away a strange prickle of dread.

More time with Keith. She should be thrilled. After all, she was in the clear. Her crimes were behind her. She had nothing to fear. And besides, by the time she saw her neighbor again, Operation Karma Reset would be in full effect. Then, she could enjoy him with an open, guilt-free heart.

Couldn't she?

11

FALLYN

BEFORE HER FIRST DIVE, Fallyn had wondered if it might all start to feel like a chore after a while. Getting the air tanks filled, wrestling her limbs into her thick neoprene wetsuit, strapping on the heavy gear... all to throw herself into the frigid waters of the Gulf of Maine. How many dives before simply breathing underwater lost its magic?

If her feelings were ever going to shift in that direction, Fallyn realized now, that day was a long way off. Most of her happiest and most peaceful moments had taken place at least thirty feet underwater. She still loved it every bit as much as the first day. More so, really, since the water was so much warmer now than it had been in the spring. She still wore her thick wetsuit, but her dives no longer felt like plunging into a tub of ice water. Dive metrics were second nature to her now, so she wasted no energy worrying about her air supply or how much time she could spend at a given depth. Her dives had gotten longer, since she could stay under for twice as much time now before a chill started to seep into her bones.

And best of all? She had her favorite person in the world

as her dive partner. And despite spending nearly all of their time together, Fallyn wasn't beginning to tire of *him* yet, either.

On their dives, Fallyn and David spent as much time checking out undersea creatures as they did hunting for buried treasure. That said, Fallyn had sunk some of the windfall from the coins she'd found – she had sold two and kept the third as her own personal talisman – into some more equipment that could help them find gold.

Right at this moment, though, Fallyn's attention was on a massive school of herring. She and David had given themselves a day off from treasure hunting. Today's dive was purely for fun, and they were out in deeper water than they normally frequented in their grid-pattern search for long-lost treasure. Gabe had found a huge school of fish with his electronic fish finder, and stopped for them to dive in and check them out. As they watched, the herring came together into a bait ball that was quite a bit bigger than Gabe's boat. They swirled round and round like a tornado, light glinting off individual fish as they raced through the water, and the effect was hypnotizing.

Suddenly, David tapped her shoulder and pointed off to the left. A huge shadow loomed in the distance, moving steadily towards them. Fallyn's first thought was of the great white shark that had been spotted the week before in Cape Cod. David's thoughts seemed to be running along the same track, because he tapped her shoulder again and pointed up towards Gabe's boat.

But as the massive animal came closer, Fallyn realized that it was much too big to be a shark. She smiled at David and shook her head, then turned her attention back to the hulking gray shape.

Not a shark. As the creature swam closer, Fallyn recognized the long body and pale flippers of a humpback whale. She stayed where she was, utterly mesmerized, as the enormous animal went straight for the fish. It opened its mouth impossibly wide, and the skin below its jaw bulged as it took in a gargantuan mouthful of herring. Never in her life had Fallyn felt such awe.

They watched as the herring fled and the whale disappeared from sight. Only then did they surface and climb back onto the boat with a hand up from Gabe. Just as Fallyn was removing her dive belt, the whale breached. It soared through the air with impossible grace before plunging back into the water with a splash. The three tiny humans watched as the whale surfaced again, sticking its head out of the water before disappearing with a final flash of its white tail.

"That never gets old," Gabe said, sounding every bit as awestruck as Fallyn felt. "Did you see him underwater?"

"We did," Fallyn told him.

"It was the most amazing thing I've ever seen in my life," David said with quiet awe.

They went below for a quick rinse and a change of clothes. When they came back up on deck, Gabe was waiting for them with two hot thermoses.

"Do you like tomato soup? My wife made some yesterday. I thought you could use something to warm you up, the way the wind is whipping today."

"I love tomato soup," David replied.

"Awesome," Fallyn said. "Thank you so much."

"Oh, it's nothing," Gabe said, ducking his head. After a

moment, as Fallyn and Dave were sipping the delicious tomato-basil soup that Sasha had made, Gabe asked, "Hey, so, before we head back... could I talk to you for a minute?"

"Of course," Fallyn said. "What did you want to talk about?"

"Well, I don't want to overstep," he said hesitantly, "but there's something I've been thinking about. I'm not trying to impose or take over or anything... but I have this idea that I think might help." He led them over to a map of the gulf and pointed out the area that they had been searching in. "You've been looking here, right? But I did a bit of reading about the wreck, and if *I* was the captain in a storm like that, I would have tried to get the ship to land as soon as possible, to avoid the danger. He would have seen the storm coming and veered off. So I was thinking that, based on where you found the coins, it's likely that the ship was headed for this harbor, here." He pointed to a spot south of where they had been looking. "Basically, the captain could've gone away from the planned path, in a gambit for this harbor that was closer, as soon as possible. The currents and everything would've made sense for it, you know? The tides that day. Which means that you should be searching a bit further south, probably even southwest, instead of working your way north."

"But there's no harbor there," Fallyn said.

"There's no marina there now, but it was a common safe harbor back in the day. I read that it was even used as a smuggler's cove from time to time."

"That's really interesting." She looked at the map for a long while, studying the area that he had pointed out. "You're right, that makes complete sense. It couldn't hurt to try the area south of where we found those coins instead."

"We should take a second look at the area directly around it too," David said, "now that you have a better metal detector. There might be something there that was buried just a bit too deep for your old one to find."

Fallyn looked into David's eyes and smiled. "That's a good point."

"It's gutting to think about," Gabe murmured, still looking at the map. "I think the captain did the smartest thing and got really close to saving his crew... but he didn't quite make it."

"I'm impressed, Gabe," Fallyn said. "I did my homework – months of it – but no amount of research can compare to years of experience in these waters. I'm so grateful for your help. If we do find anything, you're welcome to a cut of it."

Gabe grinned. "I was hoping you'd say that. I actually have a few other ideas."

As Gabe directed their attention back to the map with talks of tides and currents, Fallyn couldn't help but feel guilty for the secret that they were keeping from this kind young man. He had no idea that Fallyn and David were investigating his father at his mother's behest. It was a messy situation... or it would be, if he ever found out. She could only hope that Cee-cee was wrong and that Nate had nothing to do with the disappearance of Emily Addison. Cee-cee's instincts had been right in the case of her husband lying to her that night, but there could be other reasons for that. Gabe had already come to terms with his father romancing another woman while he was still married. Coming to terms with his father's complicity in the murder of a teenage girl would be something else entirely.

With any luck, this Nate Burrows thing would be a dead

end. Fallyn really liked the Sullivan clan, and this news would be akin to tossing a grenade into their den. But Fallyn had a duty to her client before their family members, and a duty to the truth, above all else. She pushed aside her feelings of guilt as she looked out over the ocean. The image of Emily's skeletal hand floating up out of that trunk was as vivid now as it had been the day Fallyn found her. There was nothing for it.

Sometimes, justice meant tossing a few grenades and just hoping for as little collateral damage as possible...

12

DEIRDRE

DEIRDRE MADE her way down the sidewalk towards The Pawn King on shaking legs. She realized that she was hardly breathing at all and forced herself to take a long, slow breath in as she adjusted her headscarf. It was so silly to feel this nervous. This wasn't her first rodeo, after all. She might have had Ned move the majority of her ill-gotten goods, but she had sold a fair amount of it herself, as well. There was nothing different about today... except for the fact that this was the last of it. Her last fence. Once these little colorless gems were gone, Deirdre would be in the clear. She would be free to move on with her life.

She had taken the diamonds out of the cufflinks that Carter had found – the gold had already gone off to be melted down – and she was twenty miles away from Bluebird Bay. Unless someone had literally followed her here, she was in the clear. The gems were pretty much untraceable. And once she got rid of these last two gems today, she could finally be done with this for good. It would mark the end of an era – and frankly, she was glad for it. Spending time with Keith had only reinforced the sensations of guilt that had been bubbling in her chest for a while now.

It had been easy enough to feel justified – even virtuous – when her focus was on the wrong that had been done to her parents and the shallow people who had cheated them out of their life savings without a second thought. But ever since leaving The Berries, Deirdre's perspective had shifted more and more. It wasn't that she felt guilty for taking things from people who didn't deserve the sickening amount of wealth that they had accumulated. It was more that she felt guilty for letting vengeance consume her to the point of neglecting her son... and everyone else in her life.

Her friends had drifted away over the years, and she hardly spoke to her little sister anymore. Even her mother was more distant with Deirdre than she used to be. All of those years of lies had taken a toll on every relationship in Deirdre's life. She could have spent those years bonding with Carter and doing some *good* in the world. Instead, she had let nearly a decade of her life – the second half of her son's childhood – be eaten up by her dubious quest for justice. It had seemed worth it, at the time. The feelings that had driven her were so strong that it hadn't felt like much of a choice at all.

The thing was, this time in a new neighborhood, and most of all, the time she'd spent with Keith, had reoriented her. Instead of feeling better than – as in, "well, I'm less evil than *them* so I'm the good one" – she felt as if she would never quite measure up. Not because of anything Keith did, but simply because he reminded her that there were people in the world whose lives were oriented entirely towards *good*. The man spent his working hours putting out fires and saving lives... then spent his spare time hiking through the woods and picking up any little bit of trash that he spotted along the trail. Deirdre admired him and loved spending time with him... but at the same time, it left her feeling like sort of a crappy person in comparison.

Despite her intention to be completely clear of her crimes by the next time she saw Keith, they had been on two more dates since their day at the lake: one long hike up a mountain that gave them incredible views of the coast, and one phenomenal dinner at a quirky burger place called Stacked that used ingredients like grass-fed bison and honey-garlic brie. Deirdre had been slow and cautious in ridding herself of the last of her stolen goods, and Keith had been persistent in his attentions. And, that slight edge of guilt and budding inferiority complex aside, Deirdre found herself eager to say yes each time her handsome neighbor asked her out.

Keith was everything that Deirdre had thought she would never find: a hero with a gentle heart and an adventurous spirit. What's more, *his* interest in *her* showed no signs of abating. He had already invited her to go camping with him, adding that Carter was welcome to bring a friend and come along if no one could come to town and look after him while they were gone.

Beyond all those wonderful things, those great-on-paper things that didn't necessarily tell you whether or not a couple had chemistry, there was an undeniable spark of electricity between them. Deirdre could feel it every time Keith took her hand – which he did at every possible opportunity – and even when he looked her in the eyes.

Deirdre pushed thoughts of her neighbor aside as she entered the pawn shop. A cheap bell jangled overhead as she pushed her way through the heavy front door. At the sound of the bell, a young man appeared from a back room and stepped up to the counter. He was the same person who was working the one other time she had come to this place, and he certainly didn't fit the pawn shop guy stereotype. Danny was fit and attractive in a crisp dress shirt and slacks, and the last time Deirdre was here, he had proved himself to be a shrewd businessman and a tough negotiator. When Deirdre sold a gold watch here in the spring, she'd wound up getting a decent price, but not nearly as much as she might have hoped.

This time, Danny had the upper hand, for sure. She would take whatever he offered, with nothing more than a perfunctory bit of haggling, for appearances. Deirdre didn't truly need the money... but she couldn't quite bring herself to toss a perfectly matched pair of diamonds in a dumpster, either. It would be enough to get the items out of her hands with a little something to show for it.

Her final fence. And then she could turn the page on this chapter once and for all.

"Good morning," Danny said. He didn't seem to remember her from last time, which was a small mercy. "What can I help you with? Buying or selling?"

"I was wondering what I might be able to get for these." Deirdre pulled the two diamonds out of her purse – they were in a tiny Ziploc bag – and handed them over. Danny took them out of the bag and studied them for a minute, looking at them through a loupe.

"These are exceptional," he admitted. "Very well matched. From a set of earrings, maybe? Or cufflinks?"

Deirdre's stomach lurched at the word, and she struggled

to keep her composure. She should have been more cautious. She should have sold more of the stolen items out of state. She *should* have thrown those stupid little rocks off of the end of Bluebird Bay pier.

"Earrings," she said quickly. "One of them broke and my grandmother kept the diamonds. She had intended to get them reset, but just never got around to it. I had wanted to do the same, just for the sake of sentimentality. But the truth is, I already have so many pieces of hers that I hardly have occasion to wear. Things that I can actually remember her wearing, you know? So, I just figured..." She shrugged and clamped her mouth shut before she could blather on any more than she just had.

"Yeah, I hear you," Danny said, still examining the diamonds. "People are slow to let go of heirlooms, but I can't see how they're doing any honor to their loved ones by letting things gather dust. Either you should enjoy them or pass them on to someone else who will. Thank it and let it go, you know?"

"I feel the same way," Deirdre said, wanting nothing so much as to be *done* with this transaction already. "There's no point hanging on to things. So, what do you think they're worth?"

Danny was a good guy. He gave her a decent price for them in the end, and with no real haggling. Let him forget her as just another woman born into wealth with no real grasp of what things were worth, rather than remembering her as the astute woman and capable seller that she was. Deirdre didn't care. She was *done*. This horrible, exciting, stressful chapter of her life was over and done with.

Deirdre left the shop, never to show her face there again.

She was scot-free and... well, not quite as *care*free as she would have hoped. Deirdre had imagined that after unloading the last of her stolen goods, she might feel weightless. Unburdened. And there was a definite exhilaration in being financially independent, along with a deep comfort in knowing that her parents and her son were all taken care of. But still, all of those good feelings were overshadowed by a persistent fear, a feeling that the other shoe would drop at any moment.

She could only hope that the feeling would fade, in time.

A bit of shopping would be a good distraction, and both her mother and sister had birthdays coming up in the near future, so Deirdre headed to the mall. She had a fat stack of cash in her purse and a burning desire to use it for some altruistic purpose. It was about time that she started looking into local charities – no grand donations that would draw attention, but a number of monthly donations across a number of organizations – but for now, some beautiful gifts for those dearest to her would have to do.

It worked surprisingly well. It wasn't the redistribution of wealth that assuaged Deirdre's conscience, so much as the simple distraction of thinking about someone other than herself. She enjoyed running her hands over cashmere sweaters and picturing how a certain color would look on her beautiful sister, envisioning the look on their mom's face when she touched the buttery fabric. In the end, she bought enough gifts for both of them to cover birthdays *and* Christmas presents this year.

Deirdre had shopped right through lunch, and she stopped in at the food court to buy herself a pretzel to tide her over until dinnertime. One of those oversized, chewy, salty food court pretzels that never failed to lift her spirits with a taste of her childhood.

Just as Deirdre accepted a warm pretzel from the girl behind the counter, she heard a familiar laugh. Her heart skipped a beat.

It couldn't be, she assured herself. It was noon on a Thursday. Carter was still in school.

All the same, she couldn't stop herself from scanning the food court seating area for the source of that burst of laughter. The place was full of teenagers, but no Carter. Of course not. Just some other boy who sounded like him. Fear had made her mind all screwy. Deirdre shook her head and took a bite of her pretzel, chunky rocks of salt and tough surface giving way to soft, warm dough inside.

And then, she saw him.

Carter was at the front of the coffee shop line, accepting some frozen espresso drink from the barista. Deirdre stared at him, frozen with the pretzel still in her mouth. His college prep summer class didn't get out for another hour. She had watched him leave that morning, books in hand. She had even packed him a lunch with his favorite sandwich, all sorts of lunch meats crammed together between two hearty pieces of sourdough. Had he ditched school entirely? Or just skipped out early? Either way, Deirdre's shock gave way to a quiet fury.

What the hell was Carter doing skipping his classes? Was it that girl? She was nowhere in sight... but there was his buddy Axel, and a couple of other familiar faces from the skate park crowd. All of the kids who *weren't* in the college prep program that Carter had elected to dedicate a portion of his summer to. He had *chosen* to take the extra course! So why was he blowing it off? And worse, why hadn't he said a thing to her about his decision? Had he just lied to her face this morning?

Deirdre spun around and made a beeline for the parking lot. She wouldn't embarrass her son by confronting him in public. Maybe school had let out early today. Maybe it was an exam day and some of the kids had finished early. Maybe he had a good reason for skipping out and he would be honest with her when she asked. Carter was a good kid. Deirdre wouldn't immediately assume the worst.

She leaned against her car as she finished her pretzel, giving the warm summer sunshine the opportunity to melt away some of the stress that had taken up permanent residence in her neck and shoulders. It did help. A bit. By the time she unlocked her car and opened the door, her stress level had gone from a nine down to a seven.

That was... something. Right?

Deirdre let out a shuddering breath as she slid behind the wheel.

It was done.

She'd finally washed her hands of this whole thing. She should be feeling like a weight was lifted. Where was the sense of pride in outsmarting the monsters that had done their level best to ruin her parents' lives? Where was the *relief* that she had expected to wash over her the moment she was free of the last bit of evidence that could have connected her to her successful string of robberies?

Instead, all she felt was sadness. Yes, she'd taken back what belonged to her family... but as she thought of Carter, she couldn't help but wonder what she'd lost in the process.

13

SARAH

Sarah heard Adam and his motorcycle from a mile away. She was in the front yard when he arrived, looking like something out of a catalog, wearing jeans and a jacket even in the summer sun. These days, Adam's good looks brought her a warm feeling of pleasure and pride instead of the frustration they had caused her during her brief stay on her brother's couch – and, well, most of her high school years.

"Ready to paint?" Adam asked in a booming voice as he bounded up the walkway. Before Sarah could answer, he pulled her into his arms and kissed her. When he finally released her, she took his hand and led him inside.

"Ready as can be," she told him, gesturing to the drop cloths that she had already set up. Sarah had spent her whole morning and an entire roll of painter's tape preparing each of the rooms that she wanted to tackle today. She had been tempted to leave the walls as they were and devote her energy to other things, but this cottage was the first home Sarah had ever lived in that was truly *hers* and hers alone. She wanted to put her mark on it in the hopes that it would really start to *feel* like hers. It was hard to believe that this lovely place wasn't just another rental or vacation home. She had spent days consulting Sasha, deliberating over colors, and painting big splotches on her walls. In the end, she'd settled on Etched Glass for her bedroom, Angelica Blush for the bathroom, and a warm shade called Paddington Buff for the living room.

"You've done all the hard work." Adam sounded impressed. "Should we tackle this front room together, first?"

"Sounds good," Sarah agreed. Adam filled a paint tray, Sarah started some music blasting on her portable speaker, and they got to work. Adam wielded a huge paint roller while Sarah painted the trickier spots with a brush. She was struck by their easy intimacy together, the casual way that Adam moved her aside when she was struggling to reach the tallest corner of the room. He moved her off of the stepladder with a soft touch to her hip and a kind word, then plucked the brush from her hand and finished the hard-to-reach spot.

That had been one of her big fears when she was deciding whether or not to leave her husband, Oliver, and move out of their shared apartment in D.C. Would she ever find that comfortable companionship again, someone with whom she could be her full and uninhibited self? It was still early days with Adam, but already they had reached a balance of comfort and excitement that she had never experienced before. How could she feel so completely safe and at home with someone who still made her heart race just by smiling at her? She didn't understand it, but there it was.

"How have things been at the shop?" she asked him when they retreated to the kitchen for a lemonade break. Adam owned his own little garage in town; he specialized in motorcycle repair but saw a good number of local cars and trucks, as well.

"It's been busy," Adam said happily. "I won't have much time to work at the start of next month. Cassandra's wedding is on the third and there will be a ton of family in town for a week on either side of that, so I don't want to be too busy to hang out with my cousins and uncles and all that. I've been working overtime this week trying to make sure I'm as free as possible when family's in town."

"That makes sense." Sarah drained the rest of her lemonade, feeling vaguely wounded. That was the third time that Adam had mentioned his cousin's wedding without inviting her. She was trying not to take it personally; maybe it was a small ceremony that didn't allow its guests a plus one. Sarah didn't want to ask, for fear of spooking him. That was the price of all of this newness and excitement, she supposed. There was always a slight edge of fear and uncertainty ready to encroach on the comfort that she felt whenever she was with him.

"Refill?" Adam asked as he poured himself a second glass of lemonade.

"Yes please." Sarah held hers out.

"Oh, I keep forgetting to ask," Adam said as he filled her glass. "Chicken or fish?"

Sarah felt her face scrunch into a quizzical frown. "What?"

"For the wedding," he said casually. "Or, you know, the reception. Whatever the party after the wedding is called. I need to tell them if you want chicken or fish."

Sarah laughed, feeling the tension that had settled over her vanish in an instant.

"What?" Adam asked with a nervous laugh of his own. "Oh man, are you busy that weekend? I'm sorry, I should have asked. I didn't get a final date until a couple days ago, and it's still far enough out that I just assumed you could make it. But you don't have to–"

"Fish," Sarah interrupted him, still half laughing. She stood on tiptoe and kissed him. "I'll have the fish."

"Whatever you say, your honor." Adam leaned in for another kiss.

They cleaned up in the living room and moved on to the bedroom. As he poured out a tray of paint in the pale shade of grayish teal that Sarah had chosen for her room, Adam asked, "Are there any new developments on that family feud situation?"

Sarah let out a snort of amusement. She picked up the roller and began to apply paint on the walls in long, clean lines. It was incredible how far a single day's work went towards making a new house feel like a proper home.

"Yeah," she said to Adam, pulling her focus back to his question. "After a bit of digging, Val and I discovered that *neither one* of the survey maps they gave us is correct. According to the oldest survey we could find, the property line goes right underneath the K–" She stopped just short of giving Adam the family name and stuttered for a moment before saying, "the new shed."

Adam burst out laughing and she gave him a look. "What?"

"Sorry," he said, hopping down off of the stepladder and moving it to the next spot. "I just got this picture in my head of a shed cut down the middle, half of it left there on the property line, just out of spite."

Sarah thought of old Mr. Kelley waving his cane about and snorted. "I wouldn't put it past them."

"So what's next?" Adam asked.

"We still need to meet with the woman who retained us—"

"The woman who retained you with a basket of veggies?"

"I'll have you know, she paid us a cash retainer," Sarah said with faux haughtiness. "The vegetables were a gift."

"Objection sustained. My apologies, your honor."

Sarah shook her head at him. "You always mix up the things that the *judge* says with a second thing that makes it sound like you're talking *to* a judge." But she said it with such affection that Adam just smiled.

The small bedroom and pocket-sized bathroom went quickly, and they still had plenty of daylight left. It seemed a shame to eat dinner inside after a full day of paint fumes, so Sarah suggested that they choose a place that had outdoor seating.

"Though I suppose we should change, first," she said with a chuckle, looking down at her paint-splattered jumpsuit.

"I have a better idea," Adam said as he wrapped his arms around her. "Wine, bread, and cheese. We make a quick stop at the store and eat down at the beach."

Sarah's stomach growled. "Add in some salami and a jar of olives and we've got ourselves a deal."

"You drive a hard bargain." Adam kissed Sarah and then released her. "But you've got yourself a deal. Let's go! I'll drive. I've got your helmet in one of my saddlebags."

Sarah felt a familiar rush of adrenaline as she strapped her helmet on and climbed onto Adam's motorcycle, wrapping her arms tight around his ribcage. He had already taken her on a few rides around town and one longer ride up the coast, but that initial excitement hadn't faded a bit. It still felt fun and daring every time... which was her new normal now, apparently.

They made their supply run and then parked down by the beach near Sarah's new house. Still full of surprises, Adam pulled a beach blanket out of his saddlebag and flashed Sarah a grin. It was brand new; he had forgotten to remove the tag. They chose a spot of sand that was far away from anyone else, and he laid out the plastic-bottomed picnic blanket with a flourish.

They had a long, leisurely dinner. Adam cut the salami and cheese with his pocket knife, and they sipped their wine straight from the bottle. When they were satiated, Adam returned the blanket and their paltry leftovers to his saddlebag, and they set off hand in hand on a walk down the beach.

"I can't believe you found a place to live that's almost as amazing as you are," Adam said. "That cottage is straight out of a storybook, and this beach..." He trailed off and shook his head.

"I love it," Sarah said. "I can't believe my luck, either." She squeezed his hand, hinting that she appreciated some of the *other* windfalls that life had dealt her lately, just as much as her magical new home.

Adam said something else, but at that same moment, Sarah saw something that drove every other thought from her mind.

Was that...? It *couldn't* be. It *was!*

Martha Pettigrew and Waylon Kelley walking hand in hand down the beach.

"What?" Adam asked. Sarah realized that she had stopped walking to stare open-mouthed at Martha and Waylon. She took a deep breath... and realized that the couple had spotted *her* too. They'd released each other's hands and were now walking a few feet apart, baseball caps pulled low over their faces.

Sarah couldn't help herself. She walked straight up to them.

"Tell me you two were just arm wrestling and not holding hands," Sarah exclaimed, trying not to laugh.

"Hi Sarah," Martha muttered, sounding defeated.

"Out for a stroll?" Sarah teased. She could feel Adam at her left shoulder, wondering what the hell was going on.

"Hi, I'm Adam," he introduced himself, sticking out his hand.

"Waylon Kelley," the other man responded, shaking it.

"Kelley," Adam murmured, and then his eyes brightened. "Are you Peter Kelley's son? Didn't your dad try to tear down that statue in the park a few years ago? An old mayor, wasn't it?"

"Adam!" Sarah scolded, nudging him. But Waylon was nodding.

"The Pettigrew statue, yeah." Waylon removed his baseball cap and held it between his hands. "That was him."

"And you would be..." Adam prompted, turning to Martha.

"Martha Pettigrew," she said in that same defeated tone. Waylon reached out to her, but she shied away.

"I knew it!" Adam crowed, utterly tone deaf. "It's like Romeo and Juliet! That's so cool!"

Martha gave him a scathing look.

"I mean, you managed to survive to adulthood," Adam said with a straight face. "So... there's that."

"*What* is going on, Martha?" Sarah asked. She couldn't wait to tell Val about this latest development in the Pettigrew-Kelley saga.

"We've been... seeing each other," Martha admitted.

"I've loved Martha since I was fifteen years old," Waylon said. Martha's expression instantly softened, though there was still a great deal of pain there. He put an arm around her and continued, "I never stopped loving her. But we were young and stupid and we let our parents get in the way. I went off to college and we didn't stay in touch. It's not as if I could call her house phone or send her letters without bringing a world of trouble down on her head. By the time I came home that summer, she was already gone."

"I took a job at a summer camp to get out of that house," Martha explained, "and then I went to college in New York."

"We didn't speak for decades," Waylon continued. He looked down at Martha and said in a softer tone, "Then, she came back last year to help take care of her dad. My heart just about stopped when I saw her. As beautiful as ever. I couldn't let our families get in the way, this time."

"But our parents are old," Martha said, looking back to Sarah. "We don't want to upset them. My poor dad has forgotten just about everything *but* his stupid feud with the Kelleys, which was always the worst side of him. And it's not like he remembers what I tell him one day to the next. It would upset him all over again, every time."

"Would he even remember that Waylon's a Kelley?"

"He looks just like his dad," Martha said helplessly.

"When my dad sees him, he starts shouting. Thinks he's Peter and starts in about something that happened fifty years ago."

"I'm sorry about your dad," Sarah said. "But what about the rest of them? You don't think they might, well, chill out a little? If they knew how much you two meant to each other? It could be exactly what you need to mend the rift."

Martha shook her head, looking doubtful. "Some rifts just go too deep, Sarah."

"And it would just make things worse if they broke up," Adam said neutrally.

"Adam!" Sarah exclaimed. Waylon tightened his hold on Martha, who turned her head into the crook of his shoulder.

"Not that you would," Adam said with a comical grimace. "Sorry."

"We should get going," Martha said. "I have to be home in time for my mom to leave for her book club."

"It was good seeing you," Sarah said weakly.

"Yeah, you too," Martha lied in a flat tone. She swallowed and asked, "You won't say anything to my mother, will you?"

"Of course not," Sarah assured her. "But... maybe you should."

Martha gave her a grim smile and nodded, more in goodbye than in agreement. Waylon spoke gently to her as they walked away, but Sarah couldn't hear what he was saying. She stood and watched them go.

"They're such a sweet couple," she said quietly. "It's a shame they have to hide that."

"They don't *have* to," Adam put in. "They're choosing to stay scared."

"Aren't you just a bucket of sunshine," Sarah muttered. He just put an arm around her and kissed her on the temple.

Adam might be carefree... but even now, Sarah felt awkward seeing Adam and Todd at the same time. She still felt the need to tone things down in front of her brother; Adam was Todd's best friend long before he was Sarah's boyfriend, and the whole situation still felt a little weird. She hated that she felt like that, but family was like that sometimes.

She could only imagine how tough the whole situation was on Martha and Waylon. Adam might think that they were being foolish, that they just needed to shore up their courage... but Adam hadn't seen how far gone Mr. Pettigrew was. Sarah's heart broke for Martha, having to choose between the man she loved and the certainty of upsetting her parents, who were already under so much stress coping with her father's illness.

She hoped that there was a light at the end of the tunnel for Martha and Waylon... but just at this moment, she couldn't imagine what that might be.

14

FALLYN

David took Fallyn with him when he drove across town to return the musty box of harbor records to "Salty" Roy Davies. He had pestered her for a few days before she had finally agreed. Between her treasure-hunting obsession, working with David, and learning to bake at the inn where she still technically lived – she spent most of her time at David's place these days – she wasn't super eager to meet a retired fisherman. But David Shaw was a man who rarely pushed for much. So, when he insisted that Fallyn just *had* to meet this character of a fisherman, she relented. And, as had happened each time that she agreed to one of David's ideas, she wasn't disappointed. The man was everything that David had promised and more.

Roy lived in a picturesque old house on the coast. It still had its original wooden shingles – most of them, anyway – and they were nearly white after decades of sun and wind and salty spray from the sea. Despite this, the weathered house was as festive as a Christmas tree, festooned from top to bottom with brightly colored lobster floats, ropes, and life buoys.

When they knocked on the front door, Roy greeted them with a toothless grin. He said something unintelligible, waved them inside, and shuffled with impressive speed into a back room. David set the box of harbor records down as Fallyn admired the framed black-and-white photographs that filled an entire wall. Some of them featured a much younger "Salty" Roy Davies standing next to dead fish much larger than he was. Others looked even older than Roy himself – pictures of Bluebird Bay when it was barely a town. There was an amazing amount of history packed into that one wall.

The old man reappeared a moment later with all of his teeth, and said, "Sorry about that, folks. Can't be bothered to leave these blasted dentures in when there's no one to talk to, but I sure am glad of the company. Can I offer you anything? Maybe a cup of Ovaltine? I'm sorry, I haven't introduced myself. Who's your friend, Shaw?"

Fallyn extended her hand and introduced herself. She had expected a man of few words, not this delightfully outspoken gentleman. Roy shook her hand with enthusiasm. When she declined the mug of Ovaltine, he brought out a tin of butter cookies and three glasses of milk, all clinking with ice. They all sat down around his weathered wooden table. The inside of the house was sparsely furnished and lavishly decorated, with richly colored glass sea floats hanging all over the place. Beautiful teal balls in rope netting caught the morning light coming through the eastern windows.

Fallyn stared at them as she ate one of the blue-tin butter cookies that she had adored as a small child. Outside, the waves roared quietly against the seashore. She never wanted to leave. It was like the entirety of Bluebird Bay was conspiring to give her the sort of cosseting she had missed out on as a little girl. She stopped herself from asking, *Will you be my grandpa?* by stuffing an entire pretzel-shaped butter cookie in her mouth.

"Champagne of Maine?" Roy offered, holding out a bottle of coffee brandy.

"No, thank you," Fallyn said with her mouth full. Apparently, her mumble was unintelligible, because he poured a healthy glug of Allen's Coffee Flavored Brandy into her glass.

"Shaw?" He turned his twinkling blue eyes to David.

"Sure, why not." David accepted a bit of the coffee brandy in his glass of milk and selected a butter cookie from the tin.

"Did you find what you were looking for?" Roy asked.

"We did," David said. "Thank you."

Fallyn took to the conversation like a cliff jumper, feeling only slightly guilty. Cee-cee had instructed them not to speak to any of Nate's friends or associates... but certainly ol' Salty Davies didn't count? She could ask *him* a question without it getting back to Nate Burrows.

"Mr. Davies," she began.

"No, please," he interrupted. "Never did go by that name. Call me Roy."

"Roy," she said, "do you know Nathanial Burrows?"

"Ayut, I know Nate," Roy said easily. "I know everyone who came through that harbor regular-like. He had a whole series of boats over the years. I never forget a boat."

"Do you remember what he owned in nineteen-ninety-seven?

"Let me chew on that for a bit," Roy mused. He closed his eyes and thought for long enough that Fallyn was sure he was going to come up empty. Then, he nodded and grinned with a flash of white porcelain. "Ayut! Pretty little schooner called the Gilded Lily around that time. The finest kind of sailboat, she was. Before he sold her off for something more fancy. The man must have been in a rush to trade up, because the buyer got a whale of a deal on the old girl. It was the talk of the docks for weeks, an absolute steal. But I suppose Nate was making enough money by then that he didn't care one way or the other. Bought something twice the size of the Gilded Lily. Not nearly as pretty, but he kept it around for years. Liked to flash his money around. Hasn't changed much, I don't suppose..."

Fallyn and David had exchanged a look over the butter cookies early in his rant. When Roy quieted for a sip of his drink, Fallyn asked, "Do you remember who Nate used to take out on the boat?"

"Oh, sure. He took his wife and kids out lots of times – cute little gremlins, they were, and his wife was a real looker." He gave them a look of pure mischief, but his voice was solemn when he added, "Never could understand why a man with such a beautiful family spent so many afternoons taking young girls out on the water. Priorities all askew, if you ask me."

There was a long silence in which Fallyn and David sat stunned while Roy nibbled happily at a butter cookie.

"How old were the girls?" David asked at last.

"Hard tellin', not knowin'," Roy murmured. "They looked old enough, if you catch my meaning. Eighteen...maybe twenty, if you squinted hard enough, which is why I minded my own business. Like I always do. Never did like sticking my nose into other people's affairs." He took a long drink of his brandy-spiked milk. "Could have been nieces or cousins or something," he added, sounding utterly unconvinced.

"Did you ever see Emily Addison on his boat?" Fallyn asked quietly.

"Nope," Roy said straightaway, shaking his head. "Nope, I woulda remembered a thing like that. For sure, I woulda. Poor girl's face was all over town for years. I woulda remembered seeing her in the harbor. Never did. Why do you ask? Do you think he had something to do with that? They caught the killers, you know."

"No, no," Fallyn said. "We're just tying up some loose ends and logistics."

"Sure," Roy said agreeably, nodding... and squinting at her like he wasn't the least bit fooled. Still, he let it pass and picked up another cookie.

They passed the rest of the visit pleasantly. David was right about Roy's sea stories – he had enough to fill a book. He told them about storms he had ridden out, ports he had visited, and nets all tangled up with baitfish and hanging in a cone like a great stinking Christmas tree. Though Roy had spent most of his life lobster fishing in the Gulf of Maine, he had spent the better part of his twenties and thirties deep-sea fishing all around the world. He was just telling them about his encounter with a Tasmanian devil when he was distracted by a neighbor pulling into her driveway next door.

"We had taken shelter from a storm and decided to go ashore the next morning to stretch our legs," he told them as he peered through his living room window. "Just walked up the hill a piece to take a look around. Well, I spotted this hole in the side of a hill and heard the strangest sound. Made me wonder if an animal had been hurt in the storm, maybe, or a young one left on its own.

"I put my face right into the burrow, right, young idiot that I was," he continued as he got up and shuffled towards the door, "and what do I see but a Tazzy devil not a foot from my face. Opened its mouth nearly as *wide* as my face and made a noise like a demon dog, all snarls and spit. I just about soiled my pants, got out of that hole in the hill quick as quick. My captain nearly pissed himself too, but in his case, it was from laughing. Excuse me, won't you?"

Roy opened the door and called to his neighbor as he walked across his front yard. "Late night last night, huh, Marjorey? What time did you get in? Couldn't have been earlier than midnight."

David chuckled as they followed Roy out. "Minds his own business," he muttered.

"Always," Fallyn agreed, keeping a straight face.

Roy finished scolding his neighbor and came back to join David and Fallyn. "Heading out already?"

"We have more work to do," Fallyn said, "but thank you so much for your hospitality. Can I come back sometime soon? I would love to hear more of your old stories."

"I've got enough to share," he said agreeably.

Fallyn felt an urge to hug the little old man – and she was *not* generally a hugger – but she settled for another handshake. Roy's working days were behind him, and his hands were soft as kidskin. "It was lovely to meet you."

"You too, darlin," Roy said warmly. As Fallyn turned towards the car, she heard him tell David, "That one's a keeper, no mistake."

She kept her head turned away to hide her grin.

"Good lead," David said as he joined her in the car.

"Absolutely," Fallyn agreed. "And it's not looking great for Nate."

But as David turned out onto the main road, her mood gradually darkened. Things were looking worse and worse for the Burrows clan as a whole, and she hated to think about what the coming fallout would mean for Gabe. Fallyn had missed so much, growing up without a grandpa. Was she dooming Gabe's baby daughter to the same fate? Because it was looking more and more like she was going to need to pull the pin on the hand grenade after all... and she just wished that she could warn Gabe to take cover.

15

DEIRDRE

DEIRDRE FELT a fresh surge of rage when Carter texted her an outright lie: *Going out with some friends after school. Be home for dinner.* She even typed out a long, furious response, thumbs-a-flying... and then deleted it. Good. She took a deep breath and tossed her phone across the room; it landed on the couch with a gentle bounce.

She would wait until he got home, and she would talk to him with calm, compassionate curiosity. Reacting in anger never did a thing to help guide her son in the right direction. It did nothing but undermine their relationship... which wasn't exactly on terra firma, at the moment. So. She had to be on her best behavior tonight. And she would be. Deirde would set the tone, and in doing so she would set a good example for her son. That was the plan, at least. Lord knew the boy had the ability to bring out the worst in her sometimes... but she had time to calm down and figure out how to discuss this in a way that might actually help the situation.

But what was she going to do with all this frustrated energy, in the meantime?

In the end, she threw herself into making their dinner from scratch. Meatloaf and spring rolls. It was a bizarre combination, but they were two of Carter's favorite foods. And she already had all of the ingredients. Her anger gradually subsided as she mixed the ingredients for the meatloaf by hand. When the anger had faded, though, she felt the full force of the fear that was underneath it.

Had she failed him?

Deirdre had been only half present for her son for years, and it was both of their bad luck that she'd had no partner to pick up the slack. If there had been any warning signs during those years, Deirdre had missed them. Carter had always been such an easygoing kid and a good student. Where had this come from?

It wasn't even the skipping out on school that bothered Deirdre the most. It was the secrecy. How many times had he done this? How many times had her son lied to her face? *That* was the thought that made her feel sick to her stomach. Why hadn't he come to her with the truth of it, whatever that was? What had she done to make him feel like he had to lie to her over and over again?

At first, she had rationalized the single day's absence – after all, she had done the same and worse at Carter's age – but when she'd called the school today to check in, they had told her that he had skipped yet again. Deirdre had asked why she hadn't been notified, and the woman on the other end had read off the contact number: Carter's cell phone number. Somehow, he had switched out the contact information that Deirdre had provided when he enrolled.

That was a whole new level of predetermined deception, and it hit Deirdre like a punch to the gut.

Deirdre closed the oven door hard enough that the whole appliance rattled, and she had to take a few more deep breaths before she felt ready to julienne vegetables. As she cut the carrots and cucumbers into thin strips, she rehearsed the things that she wanted to say to her son when he got home.

The key would be approaching the subject gently. An angry confrontation would only push him farther away, and the thought of losing him terrified her. There must be something going on underneath this spree of crappy choices, and venting her frustrations on him was the last thing that would convince him to confide in her. He needed guidance, but in order to help him, she needed to regain his trust. Somewhere along her path to vigilante justice, Deirdre had lost the thread of the most important relationship in her life. If she had been more present, she might have caught on quicker to whatever was going on with Carter. Whatever it was might not have happened at all.

Deirdre shook her head and pushed the guilt away. That wasn't going to help the situation, either. Piling on the blame on either side would only make things worse. She was here to help. That was all. Starting with a couple of sauces for these spring rolls...

Carter came home right on time, just as Deirdre was plating up the food. He dropped his backpack by the front door with a thump and Deirdre looked at him, noting the slump of his shoulders and the miserable look on his face. Whatever Carter had done today instead of going to school, it didn't look like he'd had much fun. If Deirdre was holding on to any residual anger, it evaporated at the sight of her miserable, world-weary son.

What was going on with him?

"Hi sweetheart," Deirdre greeted him. "How was your day?"

"Kind of boring." Carter shrugged. "But it was okay." He shuffled into the kitchen like something undead, but perked up ever so slightly at the sight of the food that Deirdre had made. "Hey, thanks."

"Ready to eat?" she asked. The sun was still coming in bright through the window, but it was nearly seven o'clock.

"Yeah, sure." Carter grinned, but it was a poor imitation of his usual smile.

"Go wash up. You want a ginger ale?"

"Yeah, thanks."

Deirdre's nerves had erased her appetite, and she took a long drink of her own ginger ale as they sat down to dinner. She let him get a full roll down his gullet before saying anything. Then, she took another sip of her soda and took the leap. No use postponing it.

"I called your school today."

Carter froze with a second spring roll halfway to his mouth. "Yeah?"

"Yeah." Deirdre closed her mouth against any recriminations and waited for him to say something. Carter set his spring roll down and stared at his plate for a long time. When he finally spoke, he said the last thing that Deirdre had expected to hear.

"Kadence cheated on me."

Deirdre was slow to reply, and after a minute, Carter hazarded a glance in her direction.

"I'm sorry to hear that," she managed. "I, um, I suppose I had assumed that she was the reason you were skipping school."

"It's not even real school," Carter said, hunching his shoulders protectively as he withdrew his gaze. "It's just a voluntary summer program."

"Carter," she said slowly, using her steadiest Mom Voice. Her son sighed.

"I know. I should have told you. I'm sorry. And you were kind of right." Carter looked up at her with a smile that was right on the edge of tears. "I was skipping school because of her. Because seeing her and *Colton* makes me feel like puking all over my desk. I walked into class the day after she told me and saw him talking to her... and I just *bolted*, Mom. It wasn't even a decision. I just ran away and spent the whole day sitting at the beach, staring at the waves."

Very dramatic, she thought, but didn't say. Though, what did come out of her mouth was almost equally unhelpful. "Well... at least you haven't been together very long."

"Six months," he muttered.

"What?" she exclaimed, and quickly reined it in. "Oh. I didn't know that. You haven't even been going to school there that long."

"We met at the mall," he said dismally. "In the arcade. She's really good at those dancing games. And air hockey. She's good at everything," he said miserably.

"Oh. I see." Deirdre swallowed down the pain that twisted in her chest. Yet another secret. "Well, I'm sorry. I understand how painful that feeling is."

"I know I shouldn't have lied to you. But I just couldn't face going back, and telling you *why* felt like it would be too embarrassing. So I've just been hanging with some friends who didn't sign up for that stupid college prep program."

Again, Deirdre held her tongue. Her son was talking to her about his feelings and his secrets. He was helping himself to a huge slice of meatloaf. These were promising signs.

"Kadence's parents are getting divorced," Carter confided. "She's been having a hard time with it. She was talking to Colton about it – his parents split a few years ago, and she's known him since elementary school – and he was comforting her... and then he kissed her. And she kissed him back." Carter pushed the meatloaf around on his plate without eating it, looking utterly devastated. "She says that she felt bad right away and left. And she told me the next day. But the thought of her and *Colton*. Ugh. It just makes me want to hurl. I just couldn't sit in a classroom with them every day. It would feel like my skin was turning itself inside out."

It might sound like high drama, Deirdre told herself, stuffing a spring roll into her mouth, *but this is what it sounds like when your teenager reveals his innermost feelings.* She held back her commentary and gave Carter a gentle pat on the shoulder.

"I've mostly just been at the beach or the skate park with Axel and Bryce, trying to get my mind off of things." Finally, he met her eyes. Lord, but her son had such bright and beautiful eyes. Kadence was an idiot. "I'm so sorry for lying to you, Mom. I was just so embarrassed. And the more I lied, the worse I felt. I kept telling myself that today is the last day, you know? But after a while, I had missed so much that going back felt pointless. I thought maybe I could make it to the end of summer without you finding out, and then I could just start back at school like normal... but I should have told you."

"Well," she said, rubbing his shoulder again, "now you have. I appreciate that. You can tell me anything, Carter. I'm in your corner. Always." They ate in silence for a moment, and then Deirdre asked, "How did you manage to get your number listed as the one for the school, anyway?"

Carter bit back a laugh. In a cartoonishly deep voice he said, "This is Mr. Eddings."

Deirdre laughed in spite of herself, and Carter joined in. It felt cathartic. At the same time, Deirdre worried that she was sending the wrong message.

"You know you need to go back to class tomorrow, right?"

Immediately, Carter's energy shifted. "What? Why?"

"It's Friday. One day until the weekend. You can get through one day of a half-day program."

"But *why*? It's an optional program. It's stupid."

"Carter, we already paid for this class. It was your decision to go." Probably only because his secret girlfriend had enrolled, she realized now. "There are two more weeks. You need to follow through."

He muttered something under his breath and got up from the table having eaten maybe half of his usual dinner portion.

"Where are you going?" Deirdre asked.

"I said, I'm going for a walk," Carter growled. He stalked out into the summer evening sunlight, screen door banging shut behind him.

Deirdre shoved her plate away with a sigh. Was she doing the wrong thing, trying to force him to go back? What if he just started lying to her again? Was she supposed to punish him? Wouldn't that just make all of this *worse*? She needed to address the deeper issue, which was why Carter hadn't felt like he could come to her in the first place. Not with bad news *or* good. She groaned. God. Raising a teenager was going to give her an aneurysm.

She started the next chapter of the audiobook that she had going on her phone while she packed up their leftovers and did the dishes... but she wasn't following the thread of the story at all. Her thoughts were spinning round in circles, worrying over her son's first heartbreak and future prospects. The audiobook cut off mid-sentence as her phone began to ring, so Deirdre dried her hands and picked up her phone.

It was Keith.

"Hi," Deirdre answered.

"Hey," Keith said. "Are you busy?"

"Not really. Just a bit of kitchen cleanup."

"It's a quiet day at work and I thought I'd call. I wanted to hear your voice. And I was wondering when I might be able to see you again."

"My schedule's wide open," Deirdre said flatly, looking in the direction her son had fled from their heart to heart.

"You sound down." Keith's voice was gentle. "What's going on?"

"Teenager trouble." Remembering that Keith's son had been that age not too long ago, Deirdre decided to confide in him. She wandered out onto her porch, where she could see the orange-streaked sky above Keith's empty house next door. "Carter's been skipping out on the college prep courses I paid for. And lying to me about it. I think he only chose to do the program because his girlfriend was doing it – and I didn't even know that he *had* a girlfriend until they broke up. Apparently, she kissed someone else and now he can't bear to be in the same room as her."

"Oh man." Keith chuckled softly. "Their problems just get bigger as they do, don't they?"

"I guess." Deirdre had a sudden vivid memory of her five year old at bedtime, asking her what would happen to him if she died and his grandparents died. Maybe he had always been a big-problem kind of kid. "Feels like Carter's always grappled with big, scary questions. Still waters, I guess. The thing is, he always used to *come* to me with his problems. I don't know when that stopped."

"Puberty, probably. It's not your fault, Deirdre."

"I don't know about that."

"Kids make mistakes," Keith told her. "Especially at this age. You can't let the little things fester and take over your life. Resentment is poisonous."

"Are you talking about Carter or the girl who cheated on him?" Deirdre asked lightly. Underneath, his words had hit her harder than she would let on. What would her life look like now if she hadn't let her own resentments fester and take over her life? What would her relationship with her son look like?

"Either," Keith was saying. "Both. They're just kids, which can be hard to remember when they get taller than you. You know the reasoning centers of their brain don't fully mature until they're in their twenties?"

Deirdre snorted. "Is that supposed to make me feel better?"

"Maybe," Keith replied. Deirdre could hear the smile in his voice. She could picture it.

"I feel like I need to connect with him before I can really help him course correct," Deirdre mused. "I'm just not sure how."

"Laser tag?" Keith suggested.

Deirdre laughed. "He would love that. We haven't gone in years. Is there a place nearby?"

"There's a big event in the park Saturday. I don't know if they're sold out, but it's worth looking into. All the young guys are going," Keith chuckled. "Some of the older guys too, the ones with kids. I guess some company's taking over all of Bluebird Park for the day."

"That sounds like a blast. Thank you! I'll see if I can get us in."

"Anytime," Keith said warmly. A sudden longing to see him in person hit Deirdre square in the chest.

"When's your next day off?" she asked.

"Not until next week."

"Up for a hike, Monday morning, maybe?"

"Always."

"You know where to find me," she said playfully.

Deirdre hung up, and the glow of her conversation with Keith faded fast. She was plagued by thoughts of all of the moments with her son that she had missed. All of the baseball games and school plays and science fairs... the days that they were supposed to have dinner together and she just found a lonely plate in the fridge for her late at night because she had been so preoccupied with cracking safes and keeping tabs on the people who had nearly killed her father. She had missed out on the second half of Carter's childhood, and now he was nearly a man.

So... now what?

The answer hit her in a flash.

She'd messed up, and now she needed to find a way to make it right.

16

SARAH

SARAH AND VAL sat shoulder to shoulder at the used dining table that was the centerpiece of their little conference room. They were eating Cee-cee's Cupcakes and poring over the two conflicting land border surveys – plus the third one that they had dug up, the original. As an added complication, it didn't match up with either of the surveys provided by the warring parties. The differences were minor, nothing but a fraction of a percentage of the land that they owned... but enough to affect the shed that Peter Kelley had decided to build right on the property line.

Sarah slumped back in her seat and took another bite of her cupcake.

"If this Raspberry Cheese Danish cupcake doesn't put them in a good mood, I don't know what will," Sarah said with a shrug. Val didn't answer. Sarah turned to look at her and found Val holding up one finger, eyes closed in rapture. Her cheeks were puffed up like a chipmunk storing nuts for the winter. Sarah grinned as she waited patiently for Val to finish chewing.

"Oh my god, what was in that one?" Val asked. "With the bacon on top? Soooo gooood."

"She calls that one the Brunch-cake. Maple, banana, and candied bacon. I think she uses a little bit of bacon grease in the batter."

"Well, she should win an Oscar. Or a Pulitzer. Or whatever they give geniuses for being geniuses." Val stuffed the rest of the cupcake into her mouth and got up to pour herself another cup of coffee. She started a second pot brewing and looked up at the clock they'd hung above the door. "They should be here any second," she said once she'd swallowed her chipmunk-sized bite. Did you remember to bring the riot gear?"

Sarah tipped her head in a sage nod. "Pepper spray at the ready, partner."

Somehow, Val had convinced the Pettigrew and Kelley families to meet at their office for mediation. Both had given them a ridiculous list of demands and requested concessions that she and Val had largely ignored, starting with, but not limited to, them being seated at least ten feet apart, and ending with Letitia insisting that if Peter Kelley gave her that sideways, squirrely look he was always giving her, she could bosh him on the head with her purse and not get arrested for it.

It was going to be a fun morning.

"I can't stay long," Letitia said before she had even walked into the conference room. "Martha *insisted* on coming, and while I very much appreciate her support, it means that we had to have my sister come over to sit with my husband, and that woman has always been a few bees short of a bonnet, if you get my meaning. What, those Kelleys aren't even *here* yet?"

"It's five minutes til, Mrs. Pettigrew," Sarah said. Martha entered the conference room just behind her mother, looking like she'd just stepped off of a particularly sickening carnival ride.

"Would you like some cupcakes?" Val asked brightly.

"What sort of cupcakes?" Letitia sniffed.

"Cee-cee's Cupcakes!"

"That's where I got those lemon-strawberry ones, Mom," Martha said as she grabbed one of the bacon-topped cupcakes. "Remember?"

"Those were very tasty," Letitia admitted, taking a step closer.

"Raspberry Cheese Danish Cupcake?" Sarah offered, picking one up by the wrapper and holding it out to Letitia.

"I suppose I could–"

"You're blocking the door, woman!" Peter Kelley shouted.

She wasn't. Which was a small mercy, because as it was, his cane came precariously close to her head.

"Stop that!" Waylon exclaimed. "Dad, if you keep trying to use that thing as a weapon, I swear to God I am going to take it away."

"You wouldn't dare!" Peter exclaimed – but he did lower his cane to the floor.

"You can have a walker instead."

"Of all the insolent— I could beat you just as well with a walker, young man." Peter looked at Val and Sarah, pointedly ignoring the Pettigrews. "Good afternoon, ladies."

Sarah watched Waylon and Martha exchange a beleaguered, loving look over their parents' heads. Letitia was fuming, but she stayed silent while Martha bent and spoke in a low voice into her ear. She allowed herself to be coaxed to the far end of the table, where she sat and took a bite of her cupcake. Aunt Cee-cee's talents worked their magic; Sarah saw some of the tension go out of Letitia's shoulders.

Peter Kelley took the seat closest to the door, placing himself at the head of the table. His wife, a spritely little woman with curly white hair, sat at his right hand. Waylon stayed standing, leaning against the wall next to the door and staring miserably across the room at Martha – just as soon as he'd nicked his dad's cane and propped it in an out-of-reach corner. His parents were happy as clams, and just as quiet as they bit into their bacon-banana cupcakes.

"We were able to find the original survey," Val said while everyone's mouths were full. "It predates your survey by two years, Mr. Kelley. And as it turns out, neither of the surveys that you had were quite right."

"We all knew Letitia took certain liberties with her version," said Mrs. Kelley.

"That's one way to put it," Peter chortled.

Letitia's face grew red as she chewed her raspberry cupcake. Good manners seemed to be holding back a response, but she began to chew quite furiously. Just as she swallowed, Sarah jumped in.

"As far as we can tell, the new shed is *slightly* over the line–"

"I knew it!" Letitia crowed.

At the same time, Peter shouted, "Of course your dime-store lawyers would say that! This is nothing but a setup!" He threw what remained of his cupcake down on the table and looked around wildly before turning an accusing glare towards his son. "Waylon, give me my cane!"

The cane was leaning against the wall next to the door. Waylon didn't move.

"Now!" Peter demanded.

Letitia was still shouting, something half-intelligible about the Kelleys removing every piece of that shed before her end-of-summer picnic. Mrs. Kelley started to shout back with something entirely unrelated. Something about a cat? Letitia had *thrown* something at her cat?

Sarah was tempted to put her fingers in her ears and face plant onto the table. She put two fingers in her mouth instead, Aunt Anna style, and cut through the chaos with a sharp whistle. That shut them up.

"Can we proceed with some modicum of decorum?" she asked them.

Val shot her a look and then smiled at their clients. She said, "Let's not talk about the past. Let's focus on the future and how we can resolve this in a way that makes everyone happy."

"Good luck with that," Peter scoffed. "I'm keeping my shed."

"I'll knock it down myself if I have to!" Letitia exclaimed.

"My family has had to live with the god-awful stench of your terrible cooking for decades and you can't let us build a little shed on the property line?" Mrs. Kelley asked disdainfully.

Letitia's eyes popped open and she made a sound like a boiling kettle. Sarah winced and Val let out a groan as Letitia planted her hands on the table and began to rise from her seat. But she quieted as Martha grabbed her shoulder and pulled her back down.

"I'll build a twenty-foot wall if you keep it up," Peter threatened, "and see if I don't."

"Enough!" Martha shouted. She turned to her mom and said, "It's a *shed*. It's just a shed, Mom. This is ridiculous. You can't even see it from the house."

"We'll be able to in the winter time," Letitia muttered.

"Why are you wasting your energy on this?" Martha demanded. "Don't we have enough to worry about? This feud is absurd, Mom."

"But they—"

"I don't *care*," Martha said, almost pleading. "I don't care what they did before I was born." Her eyes met Waylon's, and her voice grew stronger. "This feud has cast a shadow over our whole lives. Waylon and I had to sneak off and hide in order to play together when we were kids, and we ended up not being able to so much as speak or write to each other for years, even though—" She broke off, looking terrified. Waylon nodded in encouragement; there was a look of heartbreaking hope on his face.

"I love him," Martha finished in a calm voice, looking straight into Waylon's eyes.

"No!" Letitia exclaimed.

"Yes Mom." Martha was actually *smiling* now. She looked as if an immense weight had been lifted from her shoulders. Simply speaking the truth had set her free.

Mrs. Kelley sniffed disdainfully. Under her breath she said, "Well, that's just sad."

Still looking at Martha, Waylon declared, "I want to marry her."

There was a collective gasp, and Mrs. Kelley slumped into a faint. Martha's hand flew to her mouth as she looked at Waylon in shock and joy. She dropped her hand and nodded.

"Yes," she choked out, blinking furiously to keep from crying.

Sarah looked between Martha and Mrs. Kelley, wondering if they should try to revive her... and then the older woman opened one eye, saw that no one was paying her any attention, and sat up again with a disappointed frown.

"Over my dead body," Peter growled.

Waylon walked the length of the room and took Martha's hand. They stood side by side and looked at their parents.

"This meeting is over," Martha said. "You all go home, sit down and have a good think about your behavior and what you want your lives to be like moving forward. Waylon and I are going to be together. For holidays, and birthdays, and summer picnics." She shot him a look and he smiled at her, encouraging.

"If you all want to be a part of those days too," Waylon told his parents, "you'd better figure out how to get your acts together. You hear?" They just stared at him, gobsmacked.

"I'm going to live with him," she continued, and looked back to her mom. "I'll still be there every day to help with Dad. But I'm going back to work. And I'm going to move in with Waylon. If you need help at night, we can hire a nurse."

"This isn't a discussion to have right now." Letitia shot the Kelleys a look.

"It isn't a discussion," Martha said firmly. "I'm moving out today."

And with that, she and Waylon left hand in hand. Sarah wanted to applaud. She settled for exchanging a look of exultation with Val... and mentally tucking some of those words in her back pocket in case she needs to give Todd a similar speech. He needed to stop being so weird about her and Adam.

Letitia and the Kelleys were frozen in shock for a solid minute before they began to stir and look around, somewhat abashed but trying hard not to show it. Mrs. Kelley let out an indignant sniff and said, "I've got a hair appointment anyway."

"Wouldn't want to miss that," Letitia muttered. "Pass me another cupcake, would you?"

Sarah passed her another cupcake as Mrs. Kelley fetched her husband's cane. Distantly, Sarah heard the bell over the front door jingle. *Now* what?

Martha appeared in the doorway, looking mildly embarrassed. "We just realized that we drove you all here and you don't have rides home." She cleared her throat. "But everything I said still stands. Let's go Mom."

Sarah grabbed a cupcake for herself, watching them all file out.

"I'll allow you your shed," Letitia said in a magnanimous voice. In a lower tone, she added, "But you had best keep that cat of yours out of my garden."

Martha flashed Waylon a look of amusement, and on both faces, Sarah saw pure, elated relief. As the families left, she hoped fervently that everything would go well for the happy couple. There was no way to know for sure, and they hadn't exactly "won" the case, but she hoped that she and Val had helped the two families.

And if so? That would feel as good, if not better, than some big corporate win.

17

FALLYN

FALLYN PEERED over the rim of her coffee mug and tried not to stare at David. It was no easy task, given the sexy five o'clock shadow he was rocking and the fact that he seemed to only own pajama bottoms that had no top to match.

Not that she was complaining. In fact, it was a view she could get very, very used to. More and more, she was beginning to feel like it was a view she never wanted to give up. She had been apprehensive, at first, to get into both a romantic relationship and a business partnership with the same person... who *also* happened to be her diving buddy... but so far, sharing her work life and free time with David Shaw had brought Fallyn nothing but joy.

"Keep looking at me like that and we're going to be late for our meeting," David murmured gruffly without looking up from the newspaper in front of him.

She let out a squawk as she unfolded her legs from beneath her and stood. "I swear, I have no idea how you do that."

"I'm told I have exceptional peripheral vision," he said

with a slanted smile as he met her gaze. The intensity in his eyes warmed her cheeks. "Besides, you have a heavy stare."

"Keep looking at me like that and we're going to be late for our meeting," she teased, mimicking the gruff tone that he had used. She stood and went to top up her coffee, which had gone lukewarm while she stared at the man who had more or less taken over her life.

She could feel his eyes on her as he said, "Suddenly, that doesn't seem like such a bad prospect."

Fallyn turned back around and leaned against the kitchen counter, feeling less than glamorous in David's boxers and one of his old t-shirts. The way he was looking at her said that the hand-me-downs suited her just fine. She smiled at him and said, "Stop that. You spent most of yesterday tracking the guy down with only a first name from ol' Salty. We have to go. How did you manage to find him, anyhow?"

David shrugged and looked back at his paper, turning the page. The man was the only person Fallyn knew in their generation who still read multiple newspapers every day in their actual paper format. "He sold a boat called The Gilded Lily a couple years after Emily was killed. All the same specs as Nate's boat, as far as I could tell. Unless whoever bought it from Nate turned it over real quick – and that's possible, if he sold it at a huge loss like Roy implied – this is our guy. Plus, Roy said that Nate sold it to a guy named Gus. What are the chances there were two Guses in the state of Maine in possession of two boats called The Gilded Lily?"

"Unlikely," she admitted, chuckling.

"It wasn't hard to convince him to meet, either," David said. "He said that he eats at the same diner just about every morning and we were welcome to look for him there. Apparently, he always wears a red hat with the words *"Gone Fishing"* on it."

"Alright." Fallyn sighed and tore her eyes away from her shirtless partner. "Let's get dressed and go find this lead of yours."

They found Gus *"I'll be wearing a red Gone Fishing cap"* Kryswyck seated at a booth toward the back of the little cafe. His red cap was bleached a shade closer to pink by sun and salt; it clashed horribly with his dark orange hair, which looked similarly odd against his sun-pinked cheeks. He was sipping on a frozen, milky looking drink in a massive plastic cup, scrolling through his phone as they approached.

"Mr. Kryswyck?" David asked. The man looked up, eyebrows raised.

"That's me," Gus said with an easy smile. "You're the PI?"

"Yes, I'm David Shaw. This is my partner, Fallyn." They sat down as David said, "Thank you for meeting us today."

"It was no trouble," Gus said. He seemed like one of those affable giants who wasn't affected by much. Bigger than David and probably sixty years old, Gus's copper-colored hair didn't have even a single strand of white or gray. "I'm here as often as not. If I'm on land and awake, this is where I tend to be."

A young waitress arrived at their table in a rush and greeted them with a smile. "Would you like some menus?"

"I'll just have a coffee," Fallyn said. It was possible that her years in Chicago and her more recent stay in Bluebird Bay had spoiled her; she didn't have the stomach for the type of food served in most plastic-booth diners. Just the smell of the oil banished what little appetite she'd come in with.

"Same for me," David said. "Thanks."

"Coming right up!" the girl chirped. She hurried on to the next table.

"You were interested in The Gilded Lily?" Gus asked.

"Yes," David confirmed. "Did you purchase a schooner by that name about twenty years ago?"

"Yup," Gus said cheerfully. His eyes took on a far-seeing look, and there was a sudden dreamy quality to his smile. "She was a real sweetheart. Just a beauty. Graceful."

Fallyn accepted a hot cup of coffee from their waitress with a word of thanks. What was it with men describing their boats the way they would an old lover? Her dad had friends like that, and it had always given her the creeps. No wonder they were the same men who never seemed to hold on to a wife. She wouldn't want to spend her life with someone who talked about anyone or anything that way, either.

"It was the deal of a lifetime," Gus continued, still looking off into middle distance. "Some dummy in a rush to sell her. Can't remember who, but I got word of it from a friend of a friend that she was on the market. I never would have been able to afford such a beauty otherwise, not back then. Not even now, truth to tell, the way prices have gone up. I regret letting go of her sometimes. But I fixed her up and sold her for quite a bit more than I bought her for. Financed my trip around the world, she did, on a sturdier one-man rig. Now *that* was a trip."

"Do you remember anything else about the transaction?" David asked quickly, preempting the rambling stories that were looming over the conversation like a storm cloud. "Any little detail has the potential to help our investigation."

Gus was slow to pull his thoughts back from whatever past events they had sailed off to, but after a moment, he refocused on David and nodded. "Well, sure. Let me think."

He paused and added another packet of sweetener to his iced coffee before continuing. "I remember she was in great condition, overall. Maintenance was impeccable, and she fairly gleamed. Like a new boat, really. Except there was this massive hole in the deck. Looked like someone took a sledgehammer and sawzall to it, if you ask me." He frowned and took a long sip of his drink.

A shiver ran through her as Gus continued.

"The guy told me it had been vandalized the week before and he didn't want the hassle of fixing it. That's why he was selling her so cheap."

"Do you remember anything about the man who sold you The Gilded Lily?" Fallyn asked.

"Not really." Gus shrugged. "He seemed like a nice enough guy. Boardroom type, though I suppose he must have been a decent enough sailor. He was in a hurry, I remember that. Some kind of trouble with his wife."

Fallyn felt her eyebrows shoot up. She made herself take a quick sip of coffee and kept her voice casual when she asked, "What sort of trouble?"

"I don't know, exactly. I just remember that he would only take cash, and that was a pain in the tookus. He told me that he didn't want to have to deposit a check, because then his wife would see how little he'd sold her for and there would be hell to pay. I didn't think much of it at the time, other than it being a bit of a project for me to get the time off work to go into the bank and take out all that cash. Nearly emptied my savings for the Lily, but she was worth it." Gus shrugged and took another sip of his drink. "You know how men and women sometimes have their little things they do with money, a secret stash or whatever. My ex-wife had thousands squirreled away in an urn, of all places, underneath the bag that held her mother's ashes.

"Anyway, it was none of my business. And he did have the paperwork, so..." Gus spread his hands and shrugged.

Their waitress came and set a mammoth-sized breakfast plate in front of Gus, then turned to look at David and Fallyn. "Anything else I can get for you folks?"

"We're all set," David said. "Thank you."

She walked away and David put some money on the table beneath his coffee mug.

"We'll leave you to your breakfast," he told Gus as he slid out of the booth. "Thank you very much for your time. If you could find the old paperwork from your purchase of The Gilded Lily, I'd very much appreciate a copy of that."

"I'm not sure I have it," Gus said between bites of bacon. "I got rid of nearly everything after my divorce, when I was getting ready to sail south. But I'll look. I'll scan it for you if I do find it."

"Thank you," David said. He put his business card down on the table and they said their goodbyes.

"Awfully convenient that Nate's boat was vandalized right around the time of Emily Addison's death," she said as they climbed into the car.

"Awfully," he agreed with a sage nod. "That will be an easy one for Cee-cee to confirm or deny. And the all cash thing is pretty suspicious too," David said as he started the car. "It certainly seems like Nate Burrows had something to hide."

Fallyn nodded and swallowed hard. Warring images tumbled through her mind: Gabe's smile and Cee-cee's mask of stress and worry. Old pictures of Emily's smiling face... and her blue hand floating up from the wooden trunk that Fallyn had opened deep below the waves.

"So..." she croaked as David drove them back towards Bluebird Bay, "now what?"

18

DEIRDRE

Deirdre spent most of her Friday online, researching all of the hidden gems that they had yet to discover in their new town. She had called Carter's school that morning to confirm that he had been marked present in class – thank goodness for that – and she wanted to plan them a fun-filled Saturday for them to begin to mend the damage that she had done over the years, so slowly that she hadn't even noticed their relationship eroding.

Keith's tip would make the perfect start to their day, but she wanted to fill the docket. She was glad that they had chosen Bluebird Bay as the place for Carter to finish out his high school years. It was a small, peaceful town – but it was also a popular summer tourist destination that housed dozens of fun attractions that there just wasn't enough revenue to support in most towns of that size. It was the best of both worlds, and Deirdre intended to make the most of it.

When Carter got home from his friend's house, he consented to watching a few episodes of *Firefly* – his all-time favorite show, and one that Deirdre loved nearly as much –

155

with his mom instead of retreating to his room and gaming the night away. That was something. In the morning, Deirdre let him sleep in just long enough for her to make her famous Belgian waffles. Then, she went into his room and woke him up with a gentle shake.

"Waffles are ready," she told him.

Carter groaned. "I'll have some later."

"Nope," she said firmly. "Right now. I'll make you a matcha latte for a pick-me-up."

He half opened his eyes and regarded her with an unfriendly expression. "Why right now?"

Deirdre grinned. "Because our laser tag reservations are at ten, and I don't want to miss them."

Instantly, Carter was awake. "Laser tag? Where?"

"Here in town! There's a mobile company called Laser Tag Unlimited. They're based in Portland, but they set up events all over. They're setting up a course in Bluebird Park today, and I snagged us the last two spots."

Carter grinned and rubbed the sleep from his eyes. "Yeah, okay."

She left him to get dressed. "Waffles and matcha in five!"

Laser tag was a blast. They hadn't played together since Carter was about twelve years old – and it felt like she hadn't heard him *laugh* like that since he was twelve, either. All-out belly laughing at the look on her face when he popped out from behind a tree and caught her with a laser blast that made her armor buzz. Scoring the last two spots had put them on opposite teams, which only made things more fun; they spent most of the hour targeting each other in a game of all-out, sprint-or-die Hide and Seek. The course was huge, covering both a wooded area and an open space that was filled with inflatable obstacles and climbing structures. Deirdre was winded and grateful to hear the buzz that signaled the end of the hour; Carter looked like he could have kept going all day.

"Thanks Mom," he said with a whole-hearted grin as they returned their gear. "That was wicked fun."

"The day's not over yet," Deirdre said enigmatically.

"Lunch, next?" Carter asked hopefully as they walked back to the car. "I'm starving."

She laughed. Leave it to a teenage boy to be starving two hours after downing a six-inch stack of waffles. But Deirdre knew her son well enough that she had planned for that.

"New China Buffet?" she suggested in an offhand tone.

"Um, *yes!*" Carter shot back, nearly shouting. Deirdre laughed. That place was his favorite, and they didn't go out to eat very often. When she *did* take him out to eat, though, buffets were the place. She almost felt guilty bringing him there – surely their business models depended on not having *too* many teenagers come through on any given day.

As they drove across town, Carter bouncing in his seat to the horrible music that Deirdre had allowed him to put on at full volume, she reflected on how odd it was that she still made her decisions around budget. It was a holdover habit from her childhood, in which there was never quite enough money, and her early years of motherhood, in which she had to scrimp and save for every little thing, cobbling their first home together on a wish and a prayer and planning out Carter's Christmas gifts months in advance. These days, she had enough money to take Carter to any restaurant he liked every day for the rest of his life. And yet she still opted for the

Chinese food buffet. Maybe she was still living in fear of drawing attention to herself.

Deirdre shoved her worries away. They bore reflecting on, but not today. And lucky for her, the inexpensive buffet was Carter's favorite spot in town. After they had stuffed their faces with egg rolls and orange chicken and broccoli beef, Deirdre sprang one last surprise. She had booked them an hour in a pirate-themed escape room in a gorgeous old building on the edge of town. She had been nervous about how that one would go over, but Carter was up for the challenge. And in the end, they had a fantastic time. It was exactly the sort of team-building exercise that their little two-person family needed – and even though the room recommended teams of four, they solved the whole series of puzzles, just the two of them, in fifty-five minutes.

By the time Deirdre dropped Carter at his friend Axel's house for a sleepover, she was feeling all warm and fuzzy inside. Carter was relaxed and smiling. They were on the road to building their relationship back up as strong as it had ever been. She was sure of it.

"Thanks again, Mom," Carter said. He had opened his door, but for once he was in no rush to throw himself out of the car. That was a pleasant change from him hopping out before she had even come to a complete stop. "That was a lot of fun. We haven't hung out much lately and it was really... nice."

"I had such a great time, sweetheart. Thank you for spending the day with me. What do you say we make Saturdays our day? Maybe a hike next time? There's a great burger place up north that I'd love to take you to."

"That sounds awesome," Carter said enthusiastically. "I'm in. And maybe a Portland day?"

"Absolutely. How about we take turns planning our Saturdays? We could trade off every week."

"It's a plan. I'll look up stuff to do in Portland and make reservations."

Deirdre laughed. "You're on."

"Bye Mom." He leaned over to give her an awkward, one-armed hug. Deirdre squeezed him just a little too tight, but let go as soon as he did.

"Have fun. Axel's giving you a ride home tomorrow?"

"After the beach, yeah."

"Sounds good. I'll have dinner ready."

"Thanks, Mom. Bye!"

Deirdre let out a happy sigh as she drove slowly down the street. Her contented glow faded slightly as she remembered that she had one last thing to cross off of her list today... a stop at the fire station on the way home.

"Is Keith here?" she asked when she walked in.

"Yeah," said the young man closest to her. They had been introduced at the big fundraising event, but Deirdre couldn't remember his name. He trotted off into a back room and returned with Keith, who beamed at the sight of her. He looked so handsome in a simple gray t-shirt and blue jeans. Deirdre felt a roiling mixture of attraction and dread, with no idea of how to reconcile the two.

"What a nice surprise." Keith greeted her with a hug and they walked outside together, away from the prying eyes and smirks of the younger firefighters. It was a gorgeous summer day, hot and humid without being oppressive. A refreshingly cool breeze heralded the imminent arrival of autumn. "To what do I owe the honor of this drop-in visit?" he asked her.

"I've been thinking about the fundraiser," she said awkwardly, looking off into the trees instead of meeting his eyes, "and feeling bad that I didn't contribute anything, so..." She pulled an envelope from her purse.

Keith's smile fell. "Oh, no. Deirdre, I didn't bring you here that day expecting you to donate anything. I just wanted to invite you out to a nice picnic, that's all. My own cooking skills are dismal, or I'd have made you a private feast myself."

"I know you didn't expect anything," Deirdre said, holding out the envelope until he finally took it. "It's just that it got me thinking about how I haven't given back to the community, not as much as I could. I was thinking today about how I'm still caught in the Broke Single Mom mindset, even though I haven't been hurting for money in years. And it's time that I started sharing with the community. This is as good a cause as any, don't you think?"

Surprise flashed across Keith's face as he took the envelope and felt how thick it was, and his surprise gave way to consternation when he opened it and saw that the bills were all hundreds. Deirdre had taken every penny that she had made fencing the stolen goods from her final job and put it into that envelope. Over ten grand, in all. The truth was, she was itching to get rid of it. But handing it over to Keith was probably a mistake, she thought now. The look on his face made her stomach sink. She should have made an anonymous donation somehow. What was wrong with her these days? Was she *trying* to get caught?

"This is a lot of money..." he said uncertainly. "Are you sure?"

Deirdre took a deep, steadying breath to make sure that she sounded calm and certain when she spoke. "I know." She reached out and squeezed his hand. "And I'm sure. What could be more important than saving little girls from car wrecks and house fires?"

Keith rubbed a hand across the back of his neck, looking embarrassed. "The girl in the car would have been fine. I didn't do anything but ruin the seatbelt."

"And Kelly?" Deirdre pressed. Keith had saved *that* little girl's life, no doubt about it. He just shrugged, looking bashful.

"Well," he said, still sounding doubtful, "you're a woman who knows her own mind. I'm not foolish enough to try and argue with you. And the truth is, this money will do a lot of good. Some of the hand-me-down suits those boys are wearing are criminal. This is enough money to get them properly outfitted. Thank you."

His expression was pure gratitude and...something else. Admiration?

The thought made her suddenly feel like puking.

"It's nothing."

"It's not nothing. You're an amazing woman. I don't know if I've ever met someone so generous, with such a pure heart." Every word that he said felt like another boulder dropping on her chest, and it took all she had not to wince or cut him off. "I can't believe my luck that you moved in next door."

Deirdre shook her head without meaning to.

If only he knew... A good man, an upstanding citizen like Keith, would never want to be with a thief like her. She'd spent her last year living a thousand lies, and too many of the previous ones planning how to do it. If he knew the truth of the matter, he probably wouldn't put her out if she was on fire.

Keith said something else, but his words didn't register. She couldn't take another minute of this. Mumbling something unintelligible, she turned and fled. She kept herself to a bustle until she had rounded the corner, and then she sprinted back to the safety of her car. Inside, she rested her forehead on the steering wheel and tried not to sob.

She had been a fool to think that a single donation could wipe the slate clean. She couldn't change what she'd done, but she also couldn't build a new relationship based on lies. That was no way to start this next chapter of her life. She either needed to walk away from Keith altogether, or she needed to come clean.

And frankly?

The thought of doing the latter and seeing the disgust in his face was more than she could bear.

19

SARAH

"WHAT DO YOU THINK?" Sarah asked as she parked in front of the Pettigrew house. "Cease fire or all out war?"

"Could go either way," Val said with practiced detachment. Her voice and expression were both professional and composed, but Sarah could see a glint of amusement in her eyes. "Shall we?"

Martha and Waylon's speech in their little conference room had clearly done *some* good, because Letitia and Peter each called them the next day and given them permission to come up with some sort of compromise that they could both get on board with.

"I'm not making any promises, mind," Peter had growled at the end of their call.

Letitia had finished *her* call with, "But if he thinks that we're going to let him encroach on our property without some kind of compensation, the man is dreaming!"

So... the outlook wasn't terribly promising. But Sarah and Val would do their best. They had drawn up an agreement, and today's plan was to divide and conquer. Val walked down the hill to the Kelley property while Sarah rapped on the Pettigrews' front door.

"Hello Sarah dear," Letitia greeted her in her most sugary voice. Sarah was thoroughly spooked by how Mrs. Pettigrew sounded like an entirely different person depending upon her mood. Wolf or granny – Sarah was never sure which one she was going to get. Both of them together, in any given visit, was always the most likely scenario. But she responded in kind, smiling and asking after her health.

"Oh, I've been well," Letitia said heartily as she led Sarah past the blaring television set, where Mr. Pettigrew sat staring, and through to the back porch, where she had set out iced tea and little jam-filled cookies. "Summer's my season. You should see me in the dead of winter. I have to admit, I get a wee bit prickly."

Sarah nodded along, thinking how fortunate it was that Martha had gotten *out* of that house before the weather cooled. If this powerhouse of a woman was a force to be reckoned with in the summertime, Sarah would hate to cross her in February.

"You look like you've been getting some sunshine yourself," Letitia added brightly.

"Yep." Sarah and Adam had played hooky the day before to take a long hike up the coast. They had even gone skinny dipping in the cold water of a sheltered little bay. "We've been getting those beach days in while we can. And I've been doing some yard work."

"You garden?" Letitia exclaimed, leaning in.

"Well, the house I just moved into *has* a garden. Flowers, mostly. I've been trying to learn their names and how to take care of them." The garden that she had inherited, along with the little cottage that she was leasing, was magical, and she didn't want to fail the woman who had created it by letting it fade away.

"Oh." Letitia looked disappointed. "Well. It doesn't hurt to feed the bees."

"Val and I drew up a contract," Sarah said, handing over the thin folder that she had brought. She continued to talk nervously as Letitia opened it up and looked the contract over. "It's pretty simple. If both parties agree, then the shed is allowed to stay where it is. Permanently. *And*," she hastened to add as Letitia's face darkened, "the Kelleys will have agreed never to build anything else that will encroach upon your property *or* impede your view of the water. That's a *huge* concession to make for a shed, Mrs. Pettigrew. It's a win, if you ask me."

She could only hope that Val would successfully charm the Kelleys into agreeing. Waylon had paid them a visit on his own and confided that his father had no plans to build anything else at all – and he certainly didn't intend to tear down his family home to build some three-story monstrosity when it eventually passed on to him – so it wasn't as great of a concession as it seemed. Still, it certainly outweighed the minute concession of allowing the shed that was less than a foot over the property line to stay where it was. Sarah wouldn't put it past Peter Kelley to refuse to sign out of pure spite.

"I don't know," Letitia murmured as she read the short, simple contract. "It sets a dangerous precedent, letting those Kelleys encroach upon what's rightfully ours. Give that man an inch..."

"Think of Martha," Sarah said quietly, knowing that she

was taking a risk. "Isn't it time to put unnecessary stressors behind you and let sleeping dogs lie? Doesn't she deserve a bit of peace?"

Letitia gave Sarah a haunted look before quickly smoothing her expression into something more businesslike. Still, when she spoke, there was a slight quiver to her voice. "Yes. I suppose so. I'll just go in and have Frank sign, as well. You enjoy these cookies, won't you, dear?"

Sarah relished her small victory as she looked out over the garden, nibbling her jam-filled shortbread. Her exultation cooled quickly as she listened to Letitia speak to her husband in placating tones, her words lost beneath the blaring overtones of television commercials. If Frank Pettigrew was as far gone as he seemed to be, there was dubious legality in Letitia having him put his name to a document – particularly a document that he may have been opposed to if he were mentally sound. Then again, surely Letitia knew better than anyone whether her husband was mentally fit... and what he would want if he were. That was a conundrum that Sarah didn't want to tackle today. If they stayed in touch with the Pettigrews after this, she would broach the subject of power of attorney eventually. Or guardianship, if the window of opportunity for Frank Pettigrew to legally sign away his power of attorney had already closed. That was never an easy thing to navigate, but she supposed it was something that she would have to learn how to cope with as a small-town general practice attorney.

Sarah shook her head and pushed those darker thoughts away. She had held up her side of the day and scored a small win. If Val managed the same – and prospects were decent, given that Waylon had promised to be there for the meeting to help bring his parents around – they could shut the door on this little family feud. Idly, she wondered if a little Pettigrew-Kelley would be coming onto the scene sometime soon. That might be just what the family needed to truly mend fences. Then again, fighting over time with a grandchild might only make things worse.

Just then, Val came running through Letitia's garden and up the porch steps, waving her own folder in triumph.

"Success!" she declared, snagging a cookie and sinking into a rocking chair.

"That was quick!" Sarah said.

"Waylon really did all of the work for me," Val admitted. "There was a bit of grumbling and moaning, but they signed without too much fuss."

"They signed?" Letitia exclaimed, throwing the screen door open and joining them on the porch. Almost as an afterthought, she handed her own signed copy to Sarah, who flashed Val a triumphant grin.

"Job well done," Val told her as Letitia read the identical contract, ostensibly assuring herself that it was the same as the one that she had just signed.

Sarah took another blueberry jam cookie, feeling satisfied. Their first case might have been insignificant, but they had handled it well. More than that, watching Martha and Waylon take control of their own lives had been so rewarding. Letitia handed the signed contract back to Val, nodding in satisfaction.

"We gave an inch and *took* a mile, if you ask me. I suppose a few square feet of our land is a small concession to make against that ogre of a man building any more monstrosities on our property line. You girls wait here. I have a bonus ready for you."

"It's vegetables, isn't it?" Sarah whispered as Letitia went inside.

Val laughed. "I'll take it. Remember the advice she gave me on making veggie-loaded pasta sauce? It worked! I never thought I would get my little carnivore to eat zucchini and eggplant, but now he asks for 'pasketti' every night."

As expected, their bonus was two overflowing baskets of vegetables from the garden. Sarah had to admit, Mrs. Pettigrew's vegetables *were* gorgeous. There were eggplants speckled white and lavender, tiger-stripe tomatoes, and luscious ears of sweet corn – all on a bed of zucchini that Sarah would have to offload on various family members to go through it all while it was still fresh. Letitia scolded them soundly for failing to remember the *other* baskets she had loaned them, but they promised to return them all when they brought over her copies of today's contracts.

"Mind the squash blossoms on top, there," she warned them as they lugged their heavy baskets to the car. "They're delicate. Batter them up and fry them and you'll think you're in heaven, especially if you put a bit of goat cheese in the middle. Just make sure you peek inside, first, in case there's a bee hiding in there. Beyond organic, my garden is. Perfectly safe for bees, I'm proud to say. But they do like to hide themselves away in flowers from time to time. Little mischief makers."

"Thank you for the vegetables, Mrs. Pettigrew," Val said warmly. "You grow the most beautiful tomatoes in the state."

"Well, I won't argue with that," Letitia said, looking pleased. "Heirloom seeds, that's the ticket."

"And thank you for the cookies," Sarah added. "They were delicious."

"You're very welcome, dear. Oh, and I almost forgot!" she exclaimed as they were about to climb into Sarah's car. "My cousin's in need of a lawyer, and I told him that you girls were just the ticket."

Sarah fought to keep her dismay from showing on her face as a groan threatened to rise in her throat. What now? Another family squabble? Some inheritance dispute?

"What's he need help with?" Val asked brightly.

"He's in the lobster business. Must have a dozen different boats with his name on them by now. Twice that many, for all I know. Anyhow, he's been looking to hire someone as legal counsel. A local attorney, someone he can trust. Someone with good family values, you know? He's sick of those corporate law firms charging him an arm and a leg without doing a thing for him. Anyhow, I told him that you two were just the ticket. Expect a call from him this week."

As soon as they were in the car, Val squealed with happiness. "You see? Every little job we take is going to snowball like this, just you wait and see. Before long, we'll have more business than we know what to do with."

Sarah looked at their shared calendar on her phone, which had them near to fully booked for the next two weeks. "You're right about that. We might need a receptionist sooner than we thought."

"We're on our way!" Val crowed. She got on the phone with her mom to share the good news.

Before she started the car, Sarah sent a quick text message to Adam. *Break out the champagne, because I just finished my first case!*

Adam replied immediately with a string of celebratory emojis and hearts. *Can't wait to celebrate!*

Sarah chuckled and put her phone down to drive, hope and joy swelling in her chest. For the first time in years, she felt really good about every aspect of her life – *and* the direction she was heading.

20

DEIRDRE

DEIRDRE MAY HAVE HAD second thoughts about her ill-gotten gains, but it was hard to feel any true repentance when she sat out on her parents' new deck with its full-horizon ocean view. And one million times better than the view was the joy on her parents' faces the day that they saw it for the first time, and the peace that she saw there every time that she visited. This was the last home that they would ever live in, and they were enjoying every moment.

Even so, she was plagued by doubts. Could she have bought them a place like this if she had focused on her house-flipping business instead of her quest for vengeance? Maybe not... but she could have bought them something equally lovely, maybe with a view of the forest instead of this expansive view of the coast. And it wouldn't have made any difference to them, not really. She might have spent those years working side by side with her teenage son, including him in her projects rather than sneaking off and keeping everything a secret. She could still see the hurt that would cross Carter's face each time he asked to go with her to whichever property she was working on at the time and she had to put him off or turn him away with some weak excuse – because she wasn't really going there that day at all.

Eventually, he had stopped asking.

But there was no point in second-guessing her choices now. All she could do was learn from her mistakes and keep plodding along, doing her best to be a good mother and a decent member of her community. They were doing okay – Carter was finishing out his college prep course without complaint, and he had planned an action-packed Portland adventure for their next Saturday excursion – but he still felt more distant than she would like. He wouldn't say a word about Kadence or what it was like seeing her and her friend Colton at school every day. Maybe that was inevitable for a teenage boy, but Deirdre couldn't help but feel that it was the direct result of *her* keeping so many secrets from *him* over the years. All of those years that she would never get back...

And her relationship with her son wasn't the only one to suffer. Those few dates that she had been on with Keith had held all the promise of new beginnings and years of joy... and yet, she had completely backed off. He had texted her every day since she'd seen him at the station... that is, every day until today.

After four days of her sending short replies that she was too busy to meet up, he had taken the hint. No *Good morning* or *Any plans today?* or *How about a hike?* Nothing at all.

Which was exactly what Deirdre had wanted... right?

So why couldn't she stop checking her phone? Why did she feel such overwhelming grief?

God, what if he gave up on her entirely and started seeing someone else? Deirdre could barely handle watching him walk from his house to his truck. If she had to watch some other woman going in and out of that house with him, there was nothing for it. She'd have to move.

"It's your move," her dad said gently.

"What?" Deirdre tore her gaze away from the horizon to look at the chessboard between her and her dad. She hadn't noticed that he'd taken his turn. Truth be told, she wasn't paying enough attention to the game to even realize which piece he'd moved.

The wind shifted, and Deirdre caught a whiff of blueberry pie. Her mom and Carter must have just taken it out of the oven. They had been in the kitchen all morning, baking up a storm and taking turns playing the music of their respective generations at full volume. Deirdre's mom had the patience of a saint. The smell of pie and cookies was heavenly, the day was blue and gorgeous, her three favorite people in the world were here with her... and she still felt like hammered shit. Still staring at the board without really seeing it, she let out a heavy sigh.

"I'm not beating you *that* bad, princess," her dad teased. "You can still win."

She smiled at him and leaned back in her chair. "It's not that, Dad."

He leaned back in his own chair, taking off his reading glasses and giving her a long look. "You're finally ready to get it off your chest, then?"

Deirdre's heart thumped like a skittish rabbit. Outwardly, she tried to keep her composure. "Get what off my chest? What do you mean?"

"I've followed every house you've bought and sold over the years," he told her. "As well as you've done for yourself, I know that all of them together wouldn't have paid for *this* place."

"It was my other investments," she said weakly.

"Right, that's what you told your mother. Big stock market payout, something like that? She chose to believe that. She's not stupid, your mother, but she does like to take the easy option if it means keeping the peace. Me, I'm a bit more cantankerous. And I don't think that's the truth, either. Is it, pumpkin?"

She looked away, out over the railing at the wide blue sky beyond. It was a windy day, and she could see hundreds of little whitecaps playing over the surface of the ocean.

"I would guess that the way you got that money isn't strictly legal," he continued quietly. "And my *best* guess, because I know you, is that you got it from the people who tricked me out of mine."

Deirdre looked back at her father, stunned. All of her complicated lies, all of her sneaking around... she thought that she'd hidden everything so well. "What gave it away?"

Her dad winced slightly, a look of shame creeping into his expression. "I knew as soon as I told you about that pyramid scheme collapsing, all those years ago. I told you what had happened to our life savings and I watched your face change... I saw the same look of determination you had as a little kid when our idiot neighbor told you that an eight-year-old girl couldn't win the state science fair. That same steely resolve you've always had. And right in that moment, I knew that you would seek revenge." He sighed. "I hoped that I was wrong. I hoped that you would forget. You had a son to worry about, after all. You had a business that was doing so well. But you never did anything halfway," he added with a wry smile. "As soon as you moved to that hell-pit of a neighborhood, I knew what you were about."

She felt a fresh wave of guilt. "Dad, I–"

He held up a hand, and she quieted as he continued, "Every day since, I've regretted my own weakness."

Deirdre shook her head. "Dad, no, you–"

"Now, let me finish," he said with a flash of his old fire. "Not just my weakness in falling for their scheme, but my weakness in breaking down and telling *you* about it. You never should have been involved. I never should have put that on you. I should have known better.

"But in that moment, I wasn't thinking about protecting you. I was just thinking about me and your mom, how I had lost every penny that we'd scrimped and saved for. All those hours of working overtime and clipping coupons..." He shook his head. "I was so ashamed."

"But it wasn't your fault," Deirdre said. "It was *their* fault for doing this to innocent people."

"We got greedy," he said, looking down at his hands. "We had everything we needed, and then we got greedy, and we lost it all. It was the darkest time in my life. But worst of all is what it did to you. I've been terrified for you, pumpkin."

"It's done now," she said quietly. She reached out across the chessboard to take his hand. "We're free of it. It's going to be okay."

"Is it?" he asked, looking up at her. "Because that sigh tells me you aren't free of it yet..."

It took Deirdre a second to realize what he was talking about. Then, she shook her head and summoned up a smile. "It's nothing, Dad."

"Didn't sound like nothing. What's weighing on you,

princess?"

Deirdre thought of Carter and Kadence, of how deeply it hurt her that her son wasn't willing to confide in her. And so she opened up to her wise, caring father.

"I met someone."

"And?" His eyes narrowed. "Do I need to have Louie go talk to the guy?"

"Not funny," Deirdre said, even as she laughed. "No, nothing like that. He's a great guy."

"So what's the problem?"

"I feel like he's too good for me," she admitted.

"Nonsense," her dad said immediately, sitting up straight in his seat. "Not possible."

"The fireman and the thief," she muttered, looking away. "That's an odd couple."

"That's not who you are," he said firmly. "You're a smart businesswoman and a wonderful daughter and a wonderful mother."

"And a thief," Deirdre added under her breath.

"Not anymore," her father said forcefully. "Look at me, Deirdre." She met his eyes, and he continued in a gentler voice. "The first step is admitting to yourself that you've made a mistake and vowing to do better going forward. You have the rest of your life ahead of you, pumpkin. Don't waste it on regret."

"You're right Dad." For the first time in ages, Deirdre felt a steady flame of hope in her chest. "Thanks. I love you."

"I love you too, princess. Now, come on inside."

"What about chess?" she asked playfully.

"Forget chess," said her dad with a smile. "A conversation like that one calls for a fat slice of blueberry pie."

21

DEIRDRE

CARTER WENT STRAIGHT to his room when they got home – apparently, he had an online meet-up scheduled with his friends in one of the virtual worlds that they frequented – and Deirdre found herself standing in her living room, staring at the house next door. She knew what she wanted to do. She wanted to march right over there and kiss that slow-building grin that Keith greeted her with every time that he saw her.

But what if there was no grin? What if she had already blown it?

She had given him the cold shoulder for days. And he had stopped trying to contact her. Was he offended? Did he think that the check from the fire station had been her bizarre way of saying "Sorry, but I'm not interested"?

Her insecurities didn't stop her feet from leading her to her neighbor's door... but they did keep her from knocking. Deirdre found herself pacing back and forth, trying to work up the courage to knock. Maybe it was for the best. Living next to him would only be harder if she put her heart fully on the line and lost it all. She could call it quits now, before things went too far for them to coexist side by side. She could play it safe and keep him at arm's length.

But she didn't *want* to. In fact, she was *sick* of keeping the people she cared about at arm's length.

Deirdre stopped her pacing and straightened her spine. Pulling her shoulders back and lifting her chin, she raised her fist to knock – and the door opened before she touched it. She jumped back, letting out a startled little yelp.

Keith chuckled, but there was a wary look in his eyes. "I'm sorry to startle you... but it's painful sitting in there listening to you burn a hole in my welcome mat."

Deirdre's cheeks burned. "I was about to knock."

There was that slow-building smile that made her want to launch herself into his arms. "Should I close the door and give you the chance, or...?"

She smiled back, in spite of her jittery nerves. "Can I come in?"

Keith stepped back and extended his arm towards his living room. "Please."

Deirdre didn't know what she had expected – a half furnished bachelor pad, maybe, since he spent so much time at the fire station and most of his free time outdoors – but Keith's home was beautiful. It had a very masculine vibe, with wooden walls and a broad leather sofa, but it didn't feel overly Spartan. There were maybe a dozen houseplants scattered around this room alone, and the walls were adorned with pictures of Keith and his son.

"Nice place," Deirdre said weakly. She felt even more terrified than she had standing on his front step. She pointed to a picture on the wall and said, "Is that you and your son on the Appalachian Trail?"

"Yep," Keith said softly. He was standing so close to her that she could feel the heat of his arm on hers, but she didn't turn to look at him. Instead, she turned away and pointed at a clump of dark green leaves and white flowers blooming on a corner shelf.

"Is that a peace lily?"

"Yep," he said again.

Deirdre looked down at her feet and asked, "And are these floors oak, or...?"

"Chestnut. They're the original wood floors." Then, softly, "Are you here to tell me why you stopped talking to me or to put an offer in on my house?"

Deirdre laughed nervously, still not meeting his eyes. Then, very suddenly, she was taking a shuddering breath in to stop herself from crying. Keith placed a gentle hand on her shoulder.

"What's wrong?" he asked.

She forced herself to turn and look Keith in the eyes. The kindness that she saw there nearly undid her all over again. In a rush, Deirdre said, "Look, that stuff you said to me at the station? About being such a good person, or whatever your exact words were..." She shook her head helplessly and said, "It's not true. You'll never want to be with me once you know what I've done."

Keith was smiling at her, just the faintest hint of a grin beneath his beard. Mostly, she could see it in his eyes. "What? Are you going to tell me that you robbed a bank for that donation?"

"Not a bank." Deirdre's voice was barely audible, but Keith heard her. His grin faded, but he didn't step away. Instead, he took her hand and led her over to his couch, where they both sat down. Deirdre stared down at her hands, wondering what exactly to say. She felt regret for some of the decisions that she had made, but not enough to orphan her son and spend the next ten years of her life in prison for reclaiming money that rightfully belonged to her mom and dad.

Keith didn't say a word. He just sat there silently, waiting. Watching her.

"My mom and dad are my heroes," she began, speaking quietly and spinning her grandmother's ring round and round on her finger. Its tiny diamond caught the evening sunlight coming through the window. "They worked so hard all of their lives to give my sister and me all of the things that they never had growing up. A stable home in a good neighborhood. Summer trips to lakes and beaches. A good education. They were the most wonderful parents. They still are.

"When my husband left Carter and me, just after we had bought that first fixer-upper of a house, I moved back in with my parents until I found my footing again. Even when I got the house fixed up enough for Carter and I to live there, my parents were always there for us. My dad's been to more of Carter's baseball games than I have, and my mom made the costumes for most of his elementary-school plays.

"They retired a few years ago. Or... gosh, closer to a decade now. It doesn't feel like that long." She chanced a glance at Keith, who was listening with saint-like patience to what must feel, to him, like a bizarre and rambling non sequitur. "Anyway, they had done everything right. Scrimped and saved and invested. They sold our family home and bought a smaller, fancier place in a really nice neighborhood.

And then, they made one fatal mistake. They trusted the wrong people.

"My mom and dad bought into an investment scam, and they lost everything. Their house, their dream vacation, the money they had set aside for Carter's college fund... everything. We tried to file charges, but nothing came of it. There was no way to make things right. My dad nearly lost his life. He was so ashamed." Deirdre's voice broke, and it was a moment before she was able to speak again. Even though it had been nearly a decade since that terrible day, Deirdre could hardly remember it without breaking down in tears. She had dragged her dad out of his car and out of that stinking garage herself, had knelt by his side on the front lawn and tried to control her sobs enough for the 911 dispatcher to understand what she was saying. They came so close to losing him that day.

Keith took her hand in his, eclipsing it. She wanted to pull away, to save herself the pain of him recoiling when she finally admitted what she had done... but her body had a mind of its own. She clung to him, relishing the warmth of his calloused hands.

"I had to take back what was rightfully theirs," she said quietly. "Or... I felt like I did. I was obsessed. I let vengeance eat away at me. There was no Keith in my life to tell me not to."

"Deirdre," he said quietly, but she shook her head and pressed on.

"I just wanted to get enough back from the real thieves to replenish my parents' life savings. I wanted to give them the golden years that they deserve. And I did it. I'm done. But I'm not who you think I am, Keith."

"No?" he asked gently. Strangely enough, he hadn't recoiled. His hand was warm on top of hers. How could she make him understand without giving him all the incriminating details?

"That big donation wasn't generosity, Keith. It was guilt. This summer, when I had finally finished the scheme I had planned for years... I didn't feel the elation or satisfaction that I had expected. I just felt... empty. And so disconnected from my son. My obsession with revenge had all of these... all of these ramifications that I couldn't see until it was all said and done. And I'm still trying to figure out how to deal with that. How to get back on the right track. I'm not steady or good or generous. I'm just...me."

Keith was silent for a long time, but his hand stayed right where it was. Just as she was about to plead for him to say something, he began to speak in a slow rumble that soothed her nerves.

"We haven't known each other very long," he said, looking into her eyes, "so there are plenty of things we don't know about each other. I wasn't always a firefighter. Up until about ten years ago, I was a cop."

Deirdre jumped, so startled that she nearly pulled her hand from his. But he held firm. Was that a glimmer of amusement in his smile? What was his game? Her heart was beating against her ribs like a caged bird. What had she done?

"Don't run off," he murmured. "Hear me out."

"My son needs me," she whimpered involuntarily. Immediately, she felt pathetic, but she saw nothing but compassion in Keith's eyes.

"You have nothing to fear from me, Dee."

She relaxed. Just slightly. Maybe she was crazy, but she

believed him. It was something in his voice. In his eyes. Her heart rate gradually slowed as he continued to speak.

"I grew up in Portland, and not in the best neighborhood. Around the time I left for college, my little brother got hooked on drugs. I went and found the dealer that first summer, told him to leave my brother alone... but it was no use. I wasn't there to look out for him. He overdosed not too long after that. He was just a kid."

"I'm so sorry," Deirdre said, squeezing his hand.

"I know what it's like to let a quest for revenge take over your life. That might be the whole reason I became a cop... to find people like the guy who killed my brother and put them away." He chuckled, but it was a dark sound. "Imagine my excitement when I pulled that guy over one day, years later. I thought I finally had him, but he had no drugs on him. I had to let him go. But I couldn't stop thinking about him."

Keith took a deep breath and continued, "I went so far as to swipe drugs from the evidence room and hunt the guy down. I figured if he didn't have any drugs on him that time, I'd plant some. I'd make sure he went away. Paid for what he'd done. I came so close, Dee. I had the drugs in my pocket. I had the guy in handcuffs.

"Then, I saw the booster seat in the back of his car." Keith swallowed. "I asked if he had kids. The guy told me he was married with a son. That his son saved his life. He got clean, stopped dealing. He wasn't the same person who had killed my brother. Not really. That junkie was gone. I couldn't let my need for revenge make me do something I couldn't live with. I let him go. I put the drugs back. No one ever found out."

"You clearly handled things better than I did," Deirdre said, trying not to let any bitterness creep into her tone.

"No, that's not what I'm trying to say," Keith growled. "I'm telling you all that to explain that I understand what it feels like, to be so gripped by a need for revenge that you lose sight of what's right. And to tell you that I forgave that guy for doing something bad because he *knew* he'd done wrong and wanted to change. He *had* changed. I was willing to forgive the man who was responsible for my brother's death because I believe in forgiveness and second chances. You did something you regret... and I understand why you did it. Hell, if framing that guy would have brought my brother back, I would have done it. If he were still a dealer, I would have done it. I got lucky, that's all.

"We've all done things we regret, Dee. But I stand by everything I said to you at the station that day. You *are* generous. And good, and kind, and caring. Fiercely loyal. And," he added with a crooked grin, "clearly not to be messed with."

Deirdre let out a sound that was halfway between a laugh and a sob.

"I don't need to know anything more about the mistakes you've made," Keith said. "All of that's in the past. I'd like to be a part of your future, if you'd let me."

In a rush of elation and relief, Deirdre grabbed his scruffy face and kissed him full on the mouth. The kiss was everything she'd imagined it would be, grounding and electrifying at the same time. In that moment, her fear and guilt disappeared.

"Is that a yes?" Keith asked when they came up for air.

"Yes," she said emphatically.

He smiled and kissed her again. Then, he said, "I was about to grill some ribs. Will you stay for dinner?"

"I'd love to."

He squeezed her hand and walked towards his kitchen. Deirdre followed, feeling lighter than air. She had gotten a second chance to build a life for herself... and find a new purpose. A better purpose.

And to top it all off? She had found an amazing man who wanted to be a part of that journey.

Life was good.

CEE-CEE

"Stop stressing," Anna demanded. "You're going to give yourself high blood pressure. And even worse, you're starting to make *me* nervous, now. I don't like being nervous."

Cee-cee knew her sister was trying to take the edge off, and usually, it worked. But not today.

Today, nothing was going to accomplish that feat, short of Fallyn and David telling her she was paranoid. That there was no evidence of Nate being involved with the disappearance and subsequent murder of Emily Addison.

"Please, God, let that be the case," she murmured under her breath.

The office door creaked open and Cee-cee wheeled around to face it, nausea rolling through her.

"Sorry to keep you ladies waiting. Come on in," Fallyn said, waving them from the tiny but functional waiting room into the office.

As much as she'd been in a rush to hear what the PIs had uncovered so far, it took a firm nudge from Anna to get her legs moving toward the door.

She nodded at David Shaw by way of greeting before sitting in one of the worn leather chairs across from him. Anna sat next to her as Fallyn took a seat beside David.

"Cee-cee... Do you remember a boat called The Gilded Lily?"

She wet her dry lips and nodded. "Yes." She closed her eyes for a long moment and an image floated to the surface. "Yes, I remember The Lily very well. Nate loved her. She was one of his favorites over the years."

She opened her eyes just in time to see David and Fallyn exchange a glance.

That can't be good.

"And do you recall it being badly vandalized?" Fallyn pressed gently. "It would've been around the same time that Emily went missing."

Cee-cee shook her head instantly. "Nope. No way. I'd have remembered that. That thing was his baby, and if someone did something to it, I'd have never heard the end of it. In fact, I was shocked when he—" She stilled, and then locked gazes with the woman across from her before clearing her throat and starting again. "I was shocked when he sold it, frankly. He claimed he wanted something bigger, though. That's very on-brand for Nate, so I let him do his thing. I was too busy raising little ones to argue, and the boats were always his thing, not mine."

Fallyn took a deep breath and leaned forward, laying both palms on the scarred desk between them.

"Given that information, and the information we've gathered so far—" Fallyn broke off and blew out a sigh. "Look, there's no easy way to say this, Cee-cee..."

Dread rolled over her in an all-consuming wave.

Dimly, she heard her sister's whispered, *"Uh oh,"* before Fallyn continued.

"Based on the testimony of several witnesses, David and I feel that your instincts were spot on. There's a very strong chance that your ex-husband had knowledge of Emily's murder and assisted in the disposal of her body."

Anna let out a low, long whistle as Cee-cee slumped in her seat, the breath knocked out of her.

Fallyn's voice droned on in the background, but Cee-cee only heard bits and snippets.

Circumstantial.

Gus something or other.

All cash.

Because, at the end of the day, the details didn't matter much.

What mattered was that her kids were at risk of having to see their father go to jail.

What mattered was that Nate had likely been a part of something so heinous, so terrible, that she wasn't sure he could ever truly be free of.

"So, what now?" she heard Anna ask, her tone brisk and no nonsense. "If you can lay out next steps for us, that would be really helpful."

So like Anna, ready to take the bull by the horns and wrestle it to the ground, Cee-cee thought with a shake of her head, when all she wanted to do was run away and bury her head in the sand.

"That's the thing, ma'am," David said, straightening in his seat. "Given that the killers have been apprehended, and we don't have any hard evidence of Nate's involvement in Emily's murder, we're under no obligation to report this information to the police." He held up a staying hand before continuing. "Now, that doesn't mean we can't, or that we shouldn't. It just means that your sister is our client and we take that very seriously. So we're asking, here."

All three of them turned toward Cee-cee.

"Would you like us to liaise with the police department and try to get to the bottom of exactly what Nate's part might have been in the commission of this crime?"

Was this seriously happening right now?

Was she really in a room full of people waiting for her to decide whether or not to blow up her children's lives? To alter the civil relationship she had with her ex forever? To paint her sweet Grace's grandfather with the brush of murder, a mark that would never, ever go away?

"Wh-What would happen next? If we did that?"

"Probably nothing, for a few days. Ethan would likely do a second round of interviews with the people we spoke to and then run it up the chain of command to determine whether they had enough to contact Nate and ask him some questions. It could amount to nothing."

"Or," Fallyn interjected, "it could be the beginning of a very bad situation for your ex. And the rest of your family, frankly."

Cee-cee blinked back tears as she leveled Fallyn with a stare.

"What would you do if you were me?"

Fallyn looked away and shook her head slowly.

"I'm not the right person to ask. I used to see everything in black and white, right and wrong. Now... Well, let's just say I've grown. I think you need to make this decision on your own, Cee-cee."

It wasn't too late. She could just shut out the lights, lock the mental doors, and walk away. Her kids would be none the wiser, and everything would go back to the way it was before.

Then, a mental snapshot of Emily's Addison's mother, Patty, floated to the forefront of her mind, and suddenly, she knew the truth.

Nothing could ever go back to normal. Not if Nate had any part in hurting that poor girl.

"Call Ethan," she said, her throat aching. "Show him what you've got."

And in the meantime, she'd try to figure out how the hell she was going to break this to her children.

23

DEIRDRE

DEIRDRE WAS JUST GETTING DRESSED when Keith knocked on the front door. Carter opened it and called from the front room, "Your date's here, Mom!"

"I'll be right there!" Deirdre still couldn't help but smile. Even with all of the adolescent heartbreak that her son was going through, he had seemed really good with her dating. He had never even met one of Deirdre's boyfriends before – there had been so few of them, and none that she kept around long enough to consider introducing to her son – but he had taken the news that Deirdre was dating their neighbor surprisingly well. In fact, he had pestered her on and off for years to put herself out there more. On one memorable occasion, he had even tried to set her up with his seventh-grade science teacher. It had broken her heart at the time, thinking that her son was hurting for a father figure... but maybe it wasn't that at all. Maybe he had just realized that romantic partnerships were normal, and he wanted her to have that. God, maybe her never introducing so much as a date to her son is why he never told his mom about Kadence.

She had normalized both solitude and secrecy, and it had left her son feeling like he couldn't talk to her about his first love... or his first heartbreak.

She pushed those thoughts away as she walked into the front room. Trusting Carter to go to school today was a stretch for her... but what else could she do? March him into the classroom herself? That wasn't the tone that she wanted to set in their relationship. She was trying to strengthen their bond, not stomp on it.

"Hi, Keith," she greeted him with a smile. "I just need to fill a water bottle and then I'll be ready."

"No rush," he said easily.

She turned to Carter and said, "You'll be careful on the drive to school?"

He gave her an exaggerated, toothy grin. "Yes, Mother."

"And you'll *go* to school?"

"*Yes*, Mother," he said again, holding his hand out for her car keys.

"Okay." She sighed and handed them over. Carter had just gotten his license a few months before, and she could count on one hand the number of times that he had driven her car without her there in the passenger's seat. "Your lunch is in the fridge."

"Thanks," Carter said, brightening. "Hey, is it still okay if I go to Axel's for dinner? It's pizza night. They actually make them from scratch, the crust and everything. His dad used to work at a pizza place. He can toss them in the air like a pro. It's their Friday night thing."

We need a Friday night thing, she thought, wounded. But outwardly she smiled. "Sure, that's fine."

"Thanks Mom!" He kissed her cheek and headed for the kitchen.

"Don't be too late," she called after him.

He spun around with an exaggerated frown and wagged a finger at her as he walked backwards into the next room. "You either." Then, he grinned. "You kids have fun now!"

Deirdre chuckled under her breath and looked at Keith.

"I have plenty of water for both of us." He glanced across the room to make sure that Carter was gone, then kissed her lightly in greeting.

"Great," she said, grabbing her shoes. "Let's go."

"He seems like a good kid," Keith said as they walked to his truck.

"He is," Deirdre said, and then scrunched up her nose. "Most of the time."

Keith opened her door for her, gave her a hand up, and then walked around to the driver's side. "How's he adjusting to the new school?"

"That girl threw a wrench in the works," Deirdre said as she buckled her seatbelt, "but he'll be alright. He's already made a few friends in town, so it will be easier once everyone's back in school this fall."

"What does he do for fun?" Keith asked.

"Skateboarding, lately." Deirdre trailed off and looked through the windows of her house as they drove past. "He used to be into building. Huge Lego sets, cardboard forts, that sort of thing. Honestly, I'm not sure *what* he's into now. He spends a lot of time on the computer playing games with friends from his old school, but I couldn't tell you what any of the games are called or what they're about. He's been off with his new friends a lot too."

"It's great that he made friends so quickly," Keith said.

"Yeah, I know," Deirdre said without enthusiasm.

"What's wrong, Dee?"

She flashed him a smile and said, "Nothing really. It's just that *we* used to have the fun house. All through elementary school and junior high, we had the house – well, the hou*se*s – that all of his friends wanted to come to. Mario Kart, ping pong, all sorts of board games. For two years, we even lived in a house with a basketball court and a swimming pool. The house itself was run down – you should have seen the projects I tackled with that place – but twelve-year-old Carter and his friends had a blast playing outside. After that house, we moved to The Berries... that's when Carter started spending so much time online, playing computer games with his old friends. He never connected with anyone in that neighborhood... not that I can blame him. So yeah, it's great that he's found such a nice group right away here in Bluebird Bay. But I miss the days when our house was the hub."

"Have you told him that his friends are welcome at your new place?" Keith asked.

"You know what, I haven't." Deirdre reached over and squeezed his hand. "I'll have to see what I can do to make the place more enticing to teenagers. A Christmas present that will keep them entertained through the winter, maybe. First, I want some time together, just me and him. Laser tag was a success, and we went to Portland last weekend. We had a blast."

"It's all about the quality time at this age," Keith said. "He's lucky to have you in his corner."

They drove to Acadia National Park and hiked a short, strenuous trail called the Beehive Loop. The climb was challenging, but the view from the top was one hundred percent worth it. It would have taken Deirdre's breath away – if she hadn't already been panting from the steep hike. Keith was in much better shape than she was, and even he had worked up a sweat climbing the tall hill in the summer sunshine. They had the place all to themselves, and they stayed at the top for a long while, admiring the graceful curve of the coastline and the first hints of fall color that were showing here and there amongst the green of the trees.

Keith had packed them another fantastic picnic, and so they parked at another trailhead – an easy coastal trail this time – and had lunch near the shore.

Then, since Carter had better things to do than eat dinner with his mom, Deirdre and Keith followed their day of hiking up with an early dinner at a local pub. A band came on stage just as they were finishing their food, so they ordered another round of drinks and settled in to listen.

"What would you say to one more stop on the way home?" Keith asked. "There's something I want to show you."

"I'm game," Deirdre said, still a bit buzzed from both the drinks and the dancing. Keith skirted the edge of downtown Bluebird Bay and pulled up in front of a tall old building. Summer days are long in Maine, and there was still enough light for Deirdre to see the place clearly. It was run down and uninhabited, but still a gorgeous old house. The place had three stories, not including what looked like a generous attic space up top. And almost certainly a cellar, judging by the age of the place. Late nineteenth century, maybe, or early twentieth.

"I know you had pictured a whole street full of separate houses," Keith said, "and I have no doubt that you could make that happen someday. But for now... I thought you might like to take a look at this place."

"For my community project?" Deirdre looked at him in astonishment and turned back to the house.

"The single mothers, yeah," Keith confirmed. "I suppose some of them wouldn't want to live in a shared space, but if it keeps their kids in their hometown..." Keith trailed off and shrugged. "Nearly my whole life this place was a bed and breakfast, so I know the kitchen could handle cooking for a whole crew. The backyard is pretty big too... room for a treehouse, even. The owners passed away, some time back. Their kids inherited the place all together, but no one wants to run it. But they don't want to sell it to just anyone, either. It's been sitting here for years now."

"So it's not on the market." Deirdre felt a surprising surge of disappointment.

"No," Keith said slowly. He pulled a key from his pocket. "But I told them about your idea, and they said that you're welcome to take a look at the place."

"Seriously?" Deirdre leaned over and kissed him, so excited that she got a mouthful of beard instead of finding his lips.

He chuckled and turned in his seat to kiss her properly. "You want to take a look?"

"Absolutely I do!" She was already halfway out of the car. The paint on the old building was faded and chipped, and she was already envisioning it repainted bright colors. Rainbow colors, even, like a San Francisco Victorian. Or shades of orange and yellow, like an ocean sunrise.

"You do the honors," Keith said, handing her the key. Deirdre opened the door and went in. The sitting room at the front of the house was huge, and she immediately envisioned a daycare space for kids under five. Her thoughts raced faster than she could speak, but she tried to communicate what she saw in her mind's eye to Keith, who listened with cheerful patience. She described how waist-level walls could divide the room into sections, creating safe spaces for each age group and allowing the care providers to communicate. There could be a little fort in the corner, and a miniature climbing wall for exercise on brutally cold winter days.

As they walked upstairs to explore further, Keith told her, "There are eight bedrooms in all, each with its own bathroom. I think a few of the rooms actually have two," he murmured as he opened the first door. "Yes, see? There's the sitting room and then the bedroom, there. So it could accommodate families with multiple kids easily."

"A built-in bunk bed here," Deirdre murmured, the place taking shape in her mind's eye.

"Perfect," Keith agreed. They explored each floor and discovered that the attic *was* as big as it looked from the outside. Big enough to act as a ninth bedroom or a second play space. Or maybe an office space for moms who worked online. There was a roomy office on the first floor, along with a huge kitchen and a dining room that could fit everyone all at once – especially if they added some kid-sized tables.

"Do you want to see the backyard?" Keith asked after they looked at the large root cellar.

"Definitely!"

It was twilight now, but Deirdre could see clearly enough. Or she could once she blinked the tears from her eyes. The yard was huge, and she could just see it on a summer day. They could create a huge vegetable garden, put

197

a swing set in the back corner, add a sandbox and slide... the space was perfect. It even had a perfect climbing tree that could accommodate a treehouse, just like Keith had said.

"It's everything I could have hoped for, Keith. But I don't think I could afford it."

"I think you'll find that they're obliging," he said. "It's been sitting empty for years because the siblings couldn't agree what to do with the place. A community project like this could be just the thing. Maybe name it after their folks to sweeten the deal."

"You haven't even told me their names," Deirdre said.

"The couple that ran the place for fifty years was Mr. and Mrs. Hurst," he said, and chuckled at the look on Deirdre's face, "but this place was called the Liberty Inn."

"Liberty," Deirdre said, looking out over the yard. She wrapped an arm around Keith's waist and nestled closer as he draped his arm over her shoulders. "I love it."

24

MAX

"Are you ready?" Ian asked as he walked into the bookshop. He seemed to be standing extra tall, full of energy, and beaming with excitement. Max shot him a smile and went back to counting the cash in the register.

"Just about," she said. "Two more minutes, okay?"

Ian wandered over to the muffins on display in their plastic case. "Are these up for grabs?"

"Sure," she said absently, then looked up as he grabbed one of the bacon banana bread muffins. "You don't want to wait for sushi?"

"I'll be plenty hungry for sushi, believe me." Ian grinned and wolfed down half of the muffin in one bite. "I worked through lunch today. Just barely got the room ready in time."

Max closed the register and walked around the counter. "I thought you didn't have anyone booked in that new room for another week."

"Well, yeah." Ian brushed a few crumbs from his face and leaned down to kiss her. "But I wanted it to be ready for you tonight."

Max grinned as she slipped under his arm and they walked out the door together. Ian had kept his latest escape room secret from her, as she'd requested. Usually, she helped him with the puzzles and other details, but she had so much fun solving one of his newer rooms with her family that she wanted to go through one of them from scratch again. Ian had been working on this one for weeks, and he hadn't told her a thing about it.

"Are you sure I'll be able to solve it myself?" Max asked as she locked the door behind them. "Don't your rooms take an average of four people to solve?"

"I have faith in you," Ian said warmly. "And I'll be there if you get stuck."

They drove a half hour south to their favorite sushi place, which they hadn't taken the time to do all summer. It had been a successful busy season for both of them, which was wonderful for business but left them with less time together than they would like. Max was surprised to find that she was looking forward to winter this year. They both planned to cut way back on business hours and carve out more time together, including some trips out of state.

Dinner was phenomenal. Ian went all out and turned it into a real celebration. They splashed out on sake flights, sashimi platters, fresh oysters, volcano rolls – all of their favorites. Max was so stuffed by the end of the meal that she wasn't sure she was up for an hour or more of Ian's cleverly complicated puzzles... but the drive north gave her ample recovery time. By the time they got back to Bluebird Bay, she was all fueled up and ready to tackle Ian's latest room. The only thing she knew about it was that it had a library component; she had helped him source thousands of inexpensive old books to fill the shelves, keeping any re-sellable gems for her shop.

"You've come here willingly, Beauty," Ian told her as he opened the door to the library-themed escape room. "Your father sought refuge from a storm in a mysterious palace. On his way out, he plucked a rose for you – the only thing that you would name when he offered to bring you a present from his trip abroad. But the moment your father picked the rose, he was confronted by a hideous beast. The theft of that little bit of property was a charge punishable by death.

"Your father begged forgiveness, explaining that he had committed that act only out of love for his youngest child. The beast listened, and he agreed to let the man go free and bring the rose to his daughter – but only if he sent his daughter to the palace in return. Otherwise, the beast would destroy his entire family."

"Is this Villeneuve's version?" Max asked with a smile. Ian hushed her, working to keep his face serious as a smile pulled at the side of his mouth.

"Being brave and pure of heart, you offered to go of your own free will. The beast offered you a life of luxury and amusement, with all the books you could ever read. But after a while, you grew homesick. You begged to be allowed to return home and visit your family, and the beast agreed – under the condition that you return in two months' time.

"Your father and brothers do everything they can to keep you, and succeed in detaining you longer than two months. You dream of the beast dying of despair and rush back to the palace... but he is nowhere to be found. Only you can save his life... if you can reach him in time."

Ian kissed her and stepped back through the door.

"Wait!" Max objected. "You're leaving me alone?"

He just winked and closed the door. She stomped one foot on the rug in mute protest and then started her search. It was easier than she had expected... so much so that she began to wonder if the entire room had been designed with her in mind. The clues were all literary and all hidden in battered old copies of her favorite books – starting with a variant of Beauty and the Beast in Andrew Lang's *Blue Fairy Book* – and she was able to solve most of them without even *opening* the books to find the answer. In the end, it only took her about thirty minutes to find the key that opened the second door.

When she did, Ian was kneeling at her feet. Wordlessly, he met her eyes... and smiled... and opened a tiny box. The ring inside was like nothing Max had ever seen. The band was made of thin bits of metal intricately woven together, and the stone was a rainbow explosion frozen in time.

"What is that?" she asked in astonishment.

Ian chuckled softly. "It's a black opal. Maybe a diamond would have been more self-explanatory, but I looked at a thousand different rings and I just couldn't bear to give you something so ordinary.

"Max, you're the most extraordinary person I've ever known. Just knowing you makes me a better person, and I want to be with you for the rest of our lives. Would you marry me?"

"Yes! Of course. Yes. Get up, Ian."

He jumped to his feet and pulled her into his arms. They kissed, and when he finally released her, he took the ring from its box and slid it onto Max's finger.

"Perfect fit," she said quietly, nestling closer into his chest.

Ian kissed the top of her head and squeezed her tight for a moment before letting her go. "Champagne?" he asked. "I have some in the fridge downstairs."

"Sure," Max laughed, kissing him once more before she let him go.

He turned to go and then pivoted back to her, reaching into his pocket. "Oh, here's your phone. It's been buzzing. I'll be right back." Ian's face split into a grin and he kissed her again, hard. "I love you Max."

"I love you too!" she called as he loped off down the hall. She stared after him for a minute, feeling like she was hardly attached to the ground. When he'd disappeared down the stairs, she checked her phone. There was a long series of missed calls, ending with a text from Gabe. As Max read it, her joy calcified into cold shock.

CALL ME AS SOON AS YOU GET THIS.
DAD'S BEEN ARRESTED!

Want more of the Bluebird Bay series? Pre-order Finding Purpose, coming in April of 2022!

And if you love the Sullivan family, come meet the Merrills of Cherry Blossom Point in Starting From Scratch, free with Kindle Unlimited...

Lena Merrill and Owen McEnna have been best friends for decades, and she's done a great job of pretending she's not

*in love with him that whole time...until recently. Maybe it's all
the changes in the air. Maybe it's realizing that life is passing
her by and most of her dreams are still unfulfilled. Whatever
the case, her already notoriously bad poker face is slipping, and
it needs to stop, pronto. Because there's only one thing worse
than not having Owen love her back, and that's the thought of
driving him away altogether.*

*When Nikki Merrill set off for Bluebird Bay to find her
long lost sister, Anna, she never imagined she'd be returning
home to Cherry Blossom Point with her in tow. Battle lines are
drawn when each of her siblings have wildly different
reactions to their new family member. Lena is willing to invite
Anna into their lives, Gayle and Jack can't even look at her,
and Nikki? She's caught dead in the middle of things. Will
building a relationship with her new sister splinter the one she
has with the siblings she's always known?*

*Anna Sullivan didn't want another family. Now that she
has one, though, she's in for the long haul. When she leaves
Bluebird Bay to spend some time with Nikki and meet the rest
of her siblings, she isn't prepared for the drama that ensues. It's
kind of hard to make a good impression when half of them see
her as a walking representation of their father's infidelity. And
when more family secrets are uncovered, she realizes they've
only seen the tip of the iceberg.*

*Will Anna figure out how to navigate these choppy family
waters, or will her visit to Cherry Blossom Point turn out to be
a disaster of Titanic proportions?*

Nikki Merrill stood in her kitchen, surveying the breakfast
she was making for her sister, Anna. The waffles were almost

done, the fruit was all cut, the hollandaise was finished... she just needed to poach the eggs, but that could wait until the last minute.

Might as well make a fruit compote for the waffles, she decided, pulling a bag of frozen berries from the freezer.

Okay, so maybe cooking entirely too much food for one meal was a nervous habit. But it was soothing.

She sniffed the air, rife with the scent of melted butter and maple syrup warming, and let out a sigh. God, it felt good to be in her home again after being away for so long. It had surprised her...the sense of comfort she'd felt when she'd walked in. She hadn't been at all homesick during her stay in Bluebird Bay. Sure, she had missed her daughter, but Beth was away at college anyway. And the time away from her family here had actually given her some much-needed clarity. No, she hadn't missed all that much about Cherry Blossom Point...except her kitchen.

She had to admit, it was a chef's dream. Literally. Nikki had scrimped and saved for years as she'd planned every detail of the kitchen she'd wanted her whole life. The rest of the house was a hodgepodge of generic box-store furniture and household bric-a-brac that had been left on the side of the road with a *Free* sign. The walls were bare of art, save for a few childhood photos of Beth, and the rugs were nearly worn through. It didn't usually bother her, but she had almost been embarrassed showing Anna around when they'd arrived two nights before. The dusty living room with its one yellow couch and one gray. The outdated bathroom with its pale pink tiles. Beth's bedroom, where Anna currently slept, still a garish shade of purple that Beth had chosen six years ago at the age of thirteen.

The kitchen, though?

The kitchen was the bomb, and Nikki's sanctuary. Each item had been chosen with the utmost care, and she had done most of the renovations herself. She had tiled the floor—twice, when her first efforts had been lackluster—painted the cabinets a pale dove gray, and installed each handle and knob herself. The Blue Damasco marble countertops were a work of art, and the collection of copper pots and pans hanging on the wall never failed to lift Nikki's spirits. It had taken her five years to save up for her Lacanche range, and she loved that thing like a second child. Sure, she'd taken her chef's knives and a few other essentials with her to Bluebird Bay, but lord... she had missed this kitchen.

She lifted the handle on the waffle maker, noting the pale golden color of the waffles, before closing it again. Two more minutes, tops.

She hadn't had access to this outlet in months. Rented apartment kitchenettes and slinging hash at Mo's Diner just didn't have the same feel as cooking food in her own home. And if she made enough for an army? Well, it never hurt to have some extra waffles in the freezer, just in case. Back when Beth was younger, Nikki used to make a huge batch of waffles every Sunday and just pop them into the toaster oven on weekday mornings for a quick breakfast. All the convenience of a toaster waffle, but a hundred times better.

"Coffee?" Anna asked blearily as she shuffled in.

"There." Nikki pointed past the gently steaming waffle maker to the fresh pot of coffee in the corner.

Anna poured herself a cup and went to sit at the table, scrolling through her phone while she rejoined the land of the living.

Nikki hoped that her sister hadn't been sleeping too poorly on the lumpy mattress in Beth's room... if Nikki had known that her sister was going to come stay with her, she would have been better prepared.

She watched her sister from under her lashes, noting the hazel eyes so like her own. Who would've thought just a couple months ago that Anna would be here right now? Nikki had gone to Bluebird Bay in hopes of meeting her father Eric's other daughter, who had been the product of an affair he'd had while already married to Nikki's mother. It hadn't been an easy decision to go. Her much-older brother, Jack, and his twin, Gayle, had nearly lost their minds.

"Let sleeping dogs lie, Nikki. Why bring more attention to Dad's terrible betrayal?"

Her sister Lena had been more diplomatic.

"If you need to go do it to feel settled, do it. I'm here for you."

And her father? Despite keeping the secret from them until after their mother passed out of respect for her feelings, he'd been all for it. In fact, he'd had hopes that maybe, if Nikki broke the ice and was able to actually connect with Anna in a meaningful way, he might get to meet her someday too. She hadn't been as optimistic as all that, and knew it was a risk to even try. Anna was a fifty-year-old woman with a life of her own. One she might not want disrupted by some stranger barging in on account of them sharing some of the same DNA.

Nikki had been dead right on that count. Initially, Anna had slammed the door shut on any attempts to get to know her. But she had stuck it out for weeks, hoping...waiting. She'd all but given up when Anna had finally relented and agreed to see her. Nikki had been sure it would be a one-time thing. When it had blossomed into more, she'd been ecstatic. They might live two hours apart, but by the time she'd packed up and was ready to leave Bluebird Bay, she knew she would see her sister again. Given their rocky start, she'd been satisfied with that.

So, two days ago, when Anna had told Nikki that she was going with her to Cherry Blossom Point?

Nikki was floored.

"Are you serious?" she'd asked.

"As a heart attack," Anna had replied. *"You're my sister, Nikki, and you've felt like my sister from the moment I finally let my guard down. And Beth already feels as dear to me as the nieces I've known their whole lives. You saw how she fit in on Thanksgiving. It was like the both of you had always been there. I can't imagine not having you guys in my life. I can't believe I almost missed out on that, just by being pig-headed. I want to meet my biological father. There are so many things I wish I'd said to Pop before he passed away. Things that I should have done with my mom before she got too sick to do them, adventures we could have had together...I'm too old to keep making the same mistakes, Nikki. I don't want to miss my chance to get to know our dad. I don't want to live with one more regret over what I should have done. Family comes first, and if something happened and I never got to meet him? I think it would feel like another loss, in some ways."*

As soon as Nikki had caught her breath, she'd agreed without really thinking it through. More time to get to know her funny, whip-smart, sassy older sister, who was brave in ways that Nikki could only dream of. But on the two-hour drive to Cherry Blossom Point, doubts had begun to creep in.

As they began to pass familiar buildings—and the street that their brother Jack lived on—she'd started to freak out a little.

Internally, at least.

Outwardly, she had tried to keep calm... but she was never much of a pretender.

She swallowed a sigh and cracked an egg into the swirling vinegar water. They'd been here two days and she still had no clue how to handle this part of things. Who should she tell first? Initially, she'd considered calling a family meeting. Letting them all know at once. Just rip off the band-aid in one fell swoop. Was that a terrible idea?

She'd had a nightmare about it the night before—Gayle had given her a look of withering disappointment, Jack had loomed over them all and lectured them until Nikki had started to cry, and Anna had started disintegrating, blowing away like dust.

She bit back a groan and scooped the perfectly poached egg from the water and transferred it to a paper towel.

Maybe she would call Lena first or go straight to Dad. After all, he was the one Anna had come to meet, and she was well aware that Jack and Gayle wanted nothing more than to sweep this part of their family history under the rug and had no interest in meeting her. But despite the whopper he'd managed to keep under wraps for decades, Eric Merrill had grown notorious for his inability to keep a secret in his old age. Once he knew, Jack and Gayle wouldn't be far behind.

How would he react to the daughter he had never known? With joy, Nikki hoped. And gratitude. When he'd told them about her, he'd been emotional and clearly indicated that he'd love to meet her. But would the reality of it be too much for him? And could Anna ever truly forgive him for just handing her over and walking away?

It had been a condition imposed by both parties. Nikki's mother had agreed to take Eric back if he never saw Rose or their baby again, and Anna's father had promised Rose that he would raise the baby as his own if she severed all contact with Eric.

What a mess.

But Anna was here now. That was the important thing.

Now she just needed to figure out how to break the news. Her family was expecting her back any day, and their texts and voice messages trying to nail down when that might be were getting more insistent.

Her relationship with Anna was still so new. What if her siblings acted like jerks? Nikki trusted Lena to be kind, but the twins... What if they treated Anna so poorly that she up and left? What if she wanted nothing to do with *any* of them anymore?

Anna, disintegrating until she disappeared from her life altogether.

No way, Nikki assured herself as she plated their food. She and Beth were part of Anna's family now, for better or for worse. And it was Nikki's job to let her siblings know it. Their dad only lived a few blocks away, and Cherry Blossom Point was a pretty small town. She would hate for them to hear her news from anyone else, and she was running out of time.

It had to be today.

"Breakfast," Nikki announced grimly as she approached the table.

"I'm not sure why you sound like you're about to serve

me a severed head," Anna said, setting down her phone, "but that smells amazing. You'd better stop cooking like this; I might never leave. Those meatballs you made last night were a revelation. I can't believe you made pasta from scratch."

Nikki managed a smile. "It's good to be back in my own kitchen."

"Oh wow," Anna said with her mouth full. "This sauce is to die for. Like silk."

"It came out good," Nikki agreed, and for a moment they enjoyed their food in silence.

"So," Anna said, still chewing. "What's the sitch, sis? You ready to bite the bullet yet?"

Nikki gulped and stared at her sister, feeling like a deer caught in the headlights of an oncoming car.

Anna cocked an eyebrow. "Or are we hunkering down here for the foreseeable future? It's fine, either way. I'm just trying to decide if I need to take up knitting. Maybe order Rosetta Stone and brush up on my Italian..."

"I'm not sure what you mean," she stammered, trying to get her head together and think of how to respond. Anna was all-too perceptive. Nikki should've known she couldn't put one past her.

"You're hiding me away like I'm your side chick and your wife is on a business trip."

"Ouch!" Nikki laughed and winced at the same time. "I am not!"

"It's okay, I'm not mad. But let's talk about it," Anna replied, setting her fork down and leaning back in the chair.

"Was it that obvious?" It was amazing how well her sister knew her already.

"Aside from driving to the next town over for groceries at

ten PM? Or staying inside all day yesterday to 'settle in'? Or the phone calls and texts you keep ignoring?" Anna shook her head solemnly. "Not obvious at all."

Nikki chuckled and held up a hand. "Okay, okay, I get it."

"What are you afraid of?" Anna asked. "Jack's disapproval? Gayle's anger? Upending everyone's lives? Worst case scenario here is what? Lay it on me."

Nikki pushed some food around on her plate, unable to meet Anna's gaze. "Worst case scenario is that Jack is such a complete ass that you run off and I never see you again."

"Not gonna happen," Anna responded immediately. "Next?"

Nikki looked up as a heavy layer of fear slipped away.

"I'm not here to cause trouble for him...or anyone else," Anna told her. "I just want a little time with Eric, if he'll have me. If anyone else decides they want to meet me, fine. I'm not going to force myself on them."

"Dad will be thrilled. And Lena wants to meet you. She won't say it to the twins, but I'm sure of it." Nikki almost stopped there, for fear of scaring her off, but she deserved to know what she was getting herself into.

"I just don't know about Jack and Gayle," she continued. "Jack is... difficult. He means well. I think. But he's so overbearing. Thinks he's always right, you know? There's never much room for compromise, no gray areas. And he's super bossy. To him, this secret should have stayed buried, and Gayle agreed. They said no good would come of it."

"I don't care about Jack *or* Gayle," Anna said with a shrug. "No skin off my back. I don't have any feelings toward them at all... aside from some irritation that they're stressing out my little sister." She leaned in and took a sip of coffee. "I say we get the truth out there and let the chips fall where they may," she told Nikki. "I deserve the chance to meet my dad if he wants to meet me. And if that's all that happens while I'm here, I'll consider it good." She shrugged. "I'm grateful just to have gotten the bonus sibling, to be honest."

"I'm grateful too. I just hope that Jack and Gayle don't make our lives hell."

"You're really selling the Merrill family dynamic in a big way," Anna quipped, withdrawing her hand and taking a huge bite of her waffles. "Seems like a party in a box."

"Sorry," Nikki said with a chuckle. "They're not all bad. They're just... protective."

"It's not like you live with them, Nikki. You can take space if they try to bully you."

Nikki pushed her plate aside and set her forehead on the table with a groan. "You haven't met Jack..." she muttered into her placemat.

"The way you're talking, I don't much want to," Anna said lightly. "Let him stay away if he disapproves so much. It's just as well. That way, I only have to juggle one long-lost relative at a time."

The words were barely out of her mouth when the front door swung open and banged against the wall, caught up by the howling November winds. A bundled-up figure tumbled inside. Nikki jumped up from her chair, heart pounding.

"You're home!" Teal green eyes shone bright in a face reddened by cold. Then again, Lena was nearly always pink-cheeked, whether that was from chilly weather or summer sun or simple excitement. Her curly blonde hair was a frizzled mess this morning, sticking out every which way from between her hat and scarf.

"I'm home," Nikki echoed shrilly, panic taking hold as her brain went offline.

Code red. Code red.

Dimly, she heard her sister Lena continue as she closed the door behind her and yanked off her cap.

"Your phone kept going to voicemail, so I wasn't sure if you had stayed longer in Bluebird Bay or if you'd taken a det — Oh, hi!" Lena said brightly. "I didn't realize Nikki had company."

Nikki watched in silent horror as Lena made a beeline toward Anna and then stopped short. Her head whipped toward Nikki, then to Anna, and back again.

The ever-present color leached from her face as she swayed on her feet.

"Holy cannoli."

ALSO BY CHRISTINE GAEL

Want to get an alert next time a new book is out, find out about sales or contests, and chat with Christine? Join the mailing list here!

Also by Christine Gael:

Maeve's Girls

(Standalone Women's Fiction)

Bluebird Bay

Finding Tomorrow

Finding Home

Finding Peace

Finding Forever

Finding Forgiveness

Finding Acceptance

Finding Redemption

Finding Refuge

Finding Comfort

Finding Truth

Finding Purpose

Cherry Blossom Point

Starting From Scratch

Just Getting Started

A Fresh Start

A Head Start

Starting Over

False Start

Lucky Strickland Series (Mystery/Thriller)

Lucky Break

Crow's Feet Coven (Paranormal Women's Fiction)

Writing Wrongs

Brewing Trouble

Stealing Time

Made in the USA
Middletown, DE
18 September 2023

38717111R00130